HOLD ON TIGHT

J. KENNER

Hold On Tight

by

J. Kenner

About Hold On Tight

A hard body. A dangerous past.
Meet Mr. February.

Reality-TV star and reformed bad boy Spencer Dean
doesn't trust women. Not after his fiancée, Brooke, left him
at the altar five years ago, breaking his heart and hardening his soul.

Now, Brooke is close to a deal for her own show that
will launch with the remodel of a popular Austin bar. The
problem? The network insists that Spencer step in as her
partner.

He's tried to forget her—but he can't deny that he still
wants her. More than that, he wants to punish her. And so
he agrees, but only on terms that are provocative, demanding, and wildly sensual.

It's the perfect set-up for extracting revenge. But he
doesn't expect to fall for Brooke all over again…

Revenge never looked so hot.

Hold On Tight is part of a binge read series by New York Times, USA Today, Wall Street Journal, Publishers Weekly, and #1 International bestselling author of the million copy Stark series, J. Kenner.

Each book in the series is a STANDALONE novel with NO cliffhanger and a guaranteed HEA!

But even so, you won't want to miss any in the series. Because then you can answer the question…

Who's Your Man of the Month?

Visit manofthemonthbooks.com to learn more!

Hold On Tight Copyright © 2018 by Julie Kenner

Cover design by Covers by Rogenna

Cover image by Perrywinkle Photography

ISBN: 978-1-940673-72-1

Published by Martini & Olive Books

v. 2018_1_25P

Chapter One

SPENCER DEAN STOPPED his Harley-Davidson WLA motorcycle in front of the driveway that led up the hill to Austin's dilapidated Drysdale Mansion. He'd inherited the classic World War II era bike from Richie, although maybe *inherited* wasn't the right word. Richie wasn't dead, after all. Just gone.

He'd been gone for almost fifteen years now, and Spence had long ago come to terms with the fact that his brother wasn't coming back. Nobody Spence loved ever came back. And God knew they all fucked up.

With a rough growl of irritation at his own maudlin thoughts, he killed the engine and dismounted, then walked the short distance up the cobbled drive to the gate. It was locked, of course, the real estate agent's lockbox dangling from the wrought iron.

Spencer hesitated, his head tilted back so he could take in the full majesty of the place. Or, rather, so that he could visualize the majesty that he could bring back to the stunning 1876 home. For generations, it had been the residence of the Drysdale family, movers and shakers in early Texas and Austin politics. Located at the end of an exclusive street a few miles from Austin's Capitol building, the four-thousand square foot home represented a stunning example of Second Empire architecture.

Henry Drysdale had overseen the construction personally, determined to build the perfect home for his young wife. As far as Spencer was concerned, he'd succeeded brilliantly, and the Drysdale family had occupied the home until the nineteen seventies when the last member of the family sold the property to a small hotel company for the purpose of a high-end B&B. The company had gone bankrupt, and the house had fallen into disrepair. Since then, it had changed hands dozens of times, but no owner had ever put in the time or the money to bring the place back to its original greatness.

Now the house was a sad mishmash of repairs and damage, failed renovations and odd choices. Spencer wanted to change all that. Hell, he'd wanted to breathe life back into this place ever since he and Richie had broken in when Spence was only a teen. They'd spent hours—no, days—exploring the rundown place. And while they were inside those walls, everything else fell away. It was just Spence and Richie, without the Crimson Eights pushing against them, urging Richie to slide deeper into the gang world that their father had tried so hard to shield them from.

Spencer had been fifteen when Richie had been arrested, and even after Richie was gone, Spence had come here, stealing in like a thief in the night. It had been his private place. A sanctuary. And until Brooke, he'd never brought another soul with him.

They'd made love for the first time in that house. Candles burning behind boarded-up windows. Picnic blankets thick on the floor. He'd been lost in love with her. Her intelligence and ambition humbled him. Her body excited him. Those soft curves and the way she gave herself to him with such trusting abandon.

He'd cleared the various nests and debris out of the fireplace, and they'd made a fire one winter night, risking discovery for the sake of romance. Her golden hair had gleamed in the firelight, and when she'd slowly pulled off her dress and stood before him naked and beckoning, he'd known that no man on earth had ever been luckier.

He'd never understood why she loved a guy like him. As far as he was concerned, it was a goddamn miracle. But she did, and that night he'd sworn that somehow, someway, he'd remake this house, then present Brooke with a bright, shiny jewel of a home. A mansion that was equal to her beauty. Just like Henry Drysdale had done for the woman he loved.

That dream, of course, had died five years ago.

So what the hell was he doing here now?

Wasn't that the question of the hour? He was here because this house was his great white whale. It was what he wanted, what he craved. To own it. To breathe life back into it. And, by doing so, to prove that he deserved to master it.

He'd stood in this very spot six months ago. One week after he'd moved back to Austin. And he'd decided at that moment that somehow, someway, he'd make it happen. And the fact that his finances were a goddamn mess wasn't going to stop him.

After a quick glance behind him to make sure no one was looking, he pulled out the jackknife-style lock pick kit that Richie had given him the week before the cops had taken him away. All things being equal, Spencer would rather have his brother, but as the lock on the gate clicked open, Spencer had to admit that there were times when the skills his brother taught him came in handy.

Richie might be a screw-up, but he'd always had Spencer's back. He'd been the one who'd fought to get Spencer into Trinity Academy on a full scholarship, pushing and prodding their father to fill out the applications and find recommendations. He'd taught Spencer to ride a bike and to pick a lock. Helped him frame his first house when Spence was only fourteen. Taught him how to lay brick. Richie always had been damn good with his hands.

Too bad those hands had held a gun. Wrong place. Wrong time.

Richie may have fucked up his own life, but he'd always been a champion for Spencer. Always watched his back.

Except where she was concerned.

He winced.

For years, he'd forced every thought of Brooke Hamlin out of his mind. Lately, those thoughts were fighting back. She was in his head. And, dammit, he couldn't seem to banish her.

It was because of the house, of course.

And here he was again, his mind still debating if he should buy the damn place.

Was he considering the purchase in spite of her? Or because of her? To prove he was worthy, even if she never even knew he was doing it?

No, he told himself sternly. He was doing it because he loved the house. Its bones. Its essence.

And, yes, he loved its memories.

With one quick glance toward the street, he slipped through the open gate, confident that no one had noticed him in the fading light. The house might be located near downtown, but it was the last house on a dead-end street, and the gate off the driveway was shadowed by a massive oak tree.

He pulled the gate shut behind him, making a mental note to oil the hinges once the place was his, then followed the stone path past a weed-choked garden to the kitchen door. It was locked as well, but in this case, there was no need to pick the lock. The breakfast area windows had been boarded over, but it was easy enough to pry one away from the framing, now rotten from lack of care and exposure to the elements.

He slipped inside, using his phone to illuminate the area. He'd stood in this very spot with Brooke, their hands clasped tight as rain pelted the building and flashes of lightning revealed her sweet, innocent smile.

Back then, he'd thought that pretty picture was real. Soon enough, though, he'd learned she wasn't innocent at all.

Damn her. And while he was at it, damn himself for continuing to let her fill his mind.

With a stern order to put her aside, he moved slowly through the house, seeing everything with an expert eye. The dull, scraped parquet floor. The sturdy doorway arch marred by chipped paint and various dings and gashes. The dust-covered wood of an intricately carved banister. The broken glass that littered the floor. The water stains and buckling floorboards. The wires that hung empty from the ceiling. The peeling wallpaper revealing long, brown stains.

For a moment, he simply stood there on the spongey floor, anger boiling in him that something so beautiful had been left to fade.

And that was it. The kicker. The defining moment.

No more wavering. No more considering.

Whatever deal he had to cut, whatever promises he had to make, this house was going to be his.

He turned off the flashlight feature on his phone, then pressed the button to speed dial his agent.

"They're interested," Gregory said, without preamble.

Inside, Spencer was doing mental fist-pumps. Outside, he forced himself to remain calm and business-like.

Yesterday, Spencer had told Gregory to feel out Molly and Andy, the executives in charge of his former show, *Spencer's Place*. After the debacle with his asshole financial manager, Brian, Spencer had walked away from the show, leaving enough footage for them to finish the season, but refusing to do another season until he was well and clear of the rat bastard who'd screwed him so bad financially.

That had been a year ago, and the network had been hounding Spencer ever since, telling him that they wouldn't consider him in breach of contract if he did another show. But the idea of another season in front of a camera didn't interest Spencer at all. All he'd wanted was the work, and Hollywood even sapped the fun out of that.

Spencer had never wanted to be recognized in the grocery store or discussed in the tabloids. He didn't want his personal tragedies shared on social media. He wanted to wash his hands of all of it.

And he'd gone so far as to discuss with Gregory what it would take to buy out the rest of the contract. Unfortunately for Spencer, it would take every dime left in his now-meager bank account.

Then six months ago he'd moved back to Austin, and the Drysdale Mansion had loomed before him, its potential promising him a way out along with a way to make the house his.

So yesterday, he'd called Gregory and pitched the show. *Mansion Makeover.* The terms were simple. Spencer would pay the mortgage on the house, but the show would fund the renovations.

It was a long shot, Spencer knew. And yesterday, he was prepared to walk away from the Drysdale Mansion if the network said no. Today, however, rejection would slice right through his heart. If the network declined, Spencer had no idea what he'd do; all he knew was that he'd have to figure out another way to claim the house as his own.

Which meant that Gregory's announcement that the network was interested in Spencer's proposal was pretty much the best news that Spencer had ever heard.

"They understand that title will be held in my name," he asked. "And that if they want me to do the show, they need to either fund the renovation themselves or find a sponsor for the materials and tools. I'm talking flooring, tile, glass, appliances, plumbing. The full meal deal. They understand that, right?"

"They understand," Gregory confirmed. "And they're on board."

"But?" Spencer pressed because he knew his agent well by now, and he'd heard the instant of hesitation in Gregory's voice.

"A minor detail," Gregory said, his tone suggesting it wasn't minor at all.

"Don't pull that shit with me, Gregory. Don't try to handle me or tell me what I'm supposed to think of the network's bullshit demands."

"They'll give you the show," Gregory said. "And you'll get clear title to the house."

Spencer felt his gut tighten. "But?"

"But they want *Mansion Makeover* on a new contract."

"A new contract? But I already owe them a show. Why not—"

"Because they already know what show they want you to do. And if you don't agree, they don't green light the mansion project."

"The hell with that," Spencer said. "Talk them out of it."

"How long have I been working with you? Come on, Spence, don't make me out to be an asshole. You know I've already tried that."

Fuck. "What show?"

"No idea. Just that they have a short-season show for you to do with a co-star, and it centers around remodeling a local bar. So it's there in Austin. Makes it easier."

"Dammit, Gregory. You know how I feel about all this. I want out. You want to represent me on a book deal, knock yourself out. But I'm done with being a pretty face on television."

"Then unless you have some serious dollars squirreled away, you can say goodbye to the Drysdale Mansion."

"So you're saying I'm screwed." He drew in a frustrated breath. "Shit. All I want—"

"I know what you want. I also know the situation. You don't have the money to buy out your contract. You're staring at a house that's a shithole but has the potential to be fucking amazing. And all you have to do to get that house is a short season with a partner. I don't see that as screwed, my friend. I see that as golden."

Spencer opened his mouth to argue, then closed it again. It wasn't ideal, that was for damn sure. But maybe Gregory was right. Maybe it was worth it.

"Talk to them. They're in town, and they want a meeting tomorrow. Come on, Spence. It's a small price to pay."

"Fine. I'll talk to them," he said. "What's the location? And for that matter, who are they setting me up with?"

"The location's a bar called The Fix on Sixth," Gregory said, and Spence grunted with approval. "You know it?"

"Solid place. I've gone in a couple of times for drinks and appetizers. The building's got good bones, but there's definitely room for improvement."

"Well, there you go. Something you can sink your teeth into. I'll tell them you're—"

"Who?" Spence asked, the firmly stressed syllable underscoring the import of the question. "Did they tell you who they're pairing me with?"

"Does it matter? You need this, Spence. If you want to restore the Drysdale Mansion, we both know this show is the only way it'll happen."

Warning bells sounded in his ears. "Who?" Spence repeated.

"Just go to the meeting, and—"

"Tell me who the fuck they want me working with."

"Brooke Hamlin," Gregory's voice was barely a whisper. But the name cut as sharp as a sword, and at least as deadly. "They want you to work with Brooke."

Chapter Two

BROOKE HAMLIN WATCHED as Jenna Montgomery tucked a stray lock of long, red hair behind her ear. It was just past ten at night, and customers filled The Fix on Sixth, a lively, successful bar located in downtown Austin.

Or, at least, Brooke had always assumed the bar was successful. She'd come with friends a number of times over the last few years and always found the drinks to be amazing, the food scrumptious, and the music hopping.

Then one of those friends, Amanda, had told her that the place was in trouble, and that Brooke should meet with Jenna Montgomery, a partner at The Fix, to discuss a remodel.

Now here she was, forcing herself not to wipe her sweaty palms on the gray silk blend of her designer skirt. Instead, she propped her elbows on the small two-top, conjured her most winning smile, and reminded herself to breathe.

"I'm not sure how much Amanda told you," Jenna said, "but we're basically doing a facelift on The Fix. We're stepping up an already awesome menu, and we're getting the word out to draw in new customers."

Brooke nodded, realizing that Jenna was only telling her part of the story. The way Amanda had explained it, The Fix was trying to do more than draw in new customers. In truth, the bar was pushing up against a serious financial crisis. Management was doing everything it could to keep the bar thriving, and that included sponsoring a Man of the Month calendar contest.

The bar would hold live contests every couple of weeks, and by autumn, they'd have their twelve hot men to put on a calendar to sell to the public. If it worked as intended, the contest would draw in crowds and up the bar's revenue.

But if they couldn't turn the place around and get it fully in the black by the end of the year, then the bar would close its doors, and Austin would lose a beloved venue. A place with great drinks, live music, and lots of local color.

More than that, the owners would lose their dream.

That was a fear that Brooke understood only too well. And the more she and Jenna discussed the details, the more Brooke thought that she and The Fix could help each other—and that Jenna wouldn't run screaming when Brooke described the wheels she'd already set in motion. Wheels that involved The Fix being the centerpiece of a real-estate based reality television show. A show that Brooke had already pitched despite the teensy-weensy detail of not yet having permission from anyone at The Fix itself.

Still, Brooke was prepared to prostrate herself on the ground and beg if that's what it took to convince Jenna. With luck, that wouldn't be necessary. Once it was all laid out for her, surely Jenna would see how perfect the show would be. Both for The Fix and for Brooke.

The show had pretty much dropped into Brooke's lap. And as far as she was concerned, it was a magical amulet that held the power to completely change her life. Or, more accurately, to justify her choices. To finally prove to her attorney father and surgeon mother that she knew her own mind and could run her own life.

She'd dropped out of medical school after her first year because she'd finally had enough. She was sick and tired of giving in to other people's demands, and she'd made up her mind to finally take control of her own life, thank you very much.

And Brooke's dream had always been to fix property, not people. Growing up, she'd gravitated more toward her grandfather and uncle's property development business than to either of her parents' careers. A reality that they'd written off as if she were a child playing with toys.

When she'd excelled in the sciences at college, they'd turned a deaf ear to her protests. Her father had announced that she would pursue medicine, that he was footing the bill, and that all other options were off the table. Theirs was a high-profile Austin family, after all. Appearances must be kept up.

It hadn't been pretty when she'd thrown it all back in their faces. Her father's words, not hers. But she couldn't care less about Austin society. And she definitely couldn't be a doctor when the interest wasn't there. It wouldn't be fair to her. And it certainly wouldn't be fair to whatever patient happened to wander into her office.

Now, four years after walking away from Southwestern Medical School, she'd finally turned a profit at The Business Plan, her relatively new commercial renovation company that specialized in small businesses that were open to the public. Bars, restaurants, B&Bs, and the like. It was a hell of a lot of work, but she was in the black, if barely, and her current focus was on getting more clients.

The Fix, of course, was a big part of that plan, and Brooke resisted the urge to cross her fingers as she explained it all to Jenna.

"Normally, I'm a little pricey," Brooke admitted after Jenna explained the bar's limited budget. "But I have a proposal for you. If you agree, it could work out great for both of us."

Jenna's brows rose, and she leaned back, her green eyes focused intently on Brooke. "Amanda mentioned you were looking for a high profile project."

"I was," Brooke said. "I am. And to tell you the truth, The Fix is exactly what I'm looking for."

It was more than that, Brooke thought. It was serendipity. For months, Brooke had been working her ass off, trying to be front and center in the community so that she was in the line of sight of people who might hire her.

Then she'd learned that The Design and Destination Channel was accepting proposals for an Austin-based real estate show that they wanted to get on the air quickly in order to fill a schedule gap. It needed to have a minimum of six episodes, and the deadline to submit was coming up fast.

Once the proposal was in, she'd been prepared to wait for weeks, but she'd heard back after twenty-four hours. And after an extensive phone interview, she'd received an invitation to meet two of the network's executives in a suite at The Driskill Hotel, a historic venue on Sixth Street, just a few blocks down from The Fix.

It had been a head-spinning, dream-making, life-changing kind of meeting. Because if she could land an actual television show, then she'd finally, truly be on the map. She'd garner local press, interviews, the works.

More than that, the show would air nationwide, and especially since the name of the show—*The Business Plan* —mirrored the name of her business, the exposure would be huge. And surely that would give her the clout and the contacts to tackle even more challenging projects.

And maybe—*maybe*—her father would stop looking at her like she was a failure.

That meeting had ended only five short hours ago with the execs telling Brooke that her proposal was the front-runner, and that the network wanted to green light the show. They just needed to ensure that two small conditions were met.

The problem, of course, was that the conditions weren't small at all.

"I'm so screwed," Brooke had wailed when she met Amanda at RA Sushi Bar, her favorite downtown venue for sushi and cocktails.

"In what universe?" Amanda countered. "You just said they loved your pitch."

"I told them I'd locked in The Fix. That was a complete and total lie."

Brooke had figured that a stage full of hot guys would catch the network's eye, and so she'd included The Fix and a description of the calendar contest in the proposal as an example of the kind of thing the show might use.

The network had gone apeshit over the idea, so apparently her instincts had been dead-on. But she hadn't expected things to move quite so fast. And now the network had included The Fix as a condition of the show getting made.

"I don't even meet with Jenna to talk about working with The Fix until later tonight," she told Amanda. "What if she doesn't want to work with me at all? Or if she thinks having a film crew on the property for months would be the equivalent of the seventh circle of hell?"

Amanda waved her hand dismissively. "Oh, please. Your work is amazing. Of course she'll want to work with you. And as for the show, I know Jenna, and she's no dummy. You tell her that the network and sponsors will cover the materials and your fee, and she'll be all in. Besides, you said the network wants to film the Man of the Month contest, right?"

"They want it in the background, for sure. They said it'll make for great television and be something no one's done before."

"And the show will premiere late summer or early fall?"

Brooke nodded.

"So, there you go. That kind of exposure should bring in new customers. Jenna's in marketing. She gets it. Trust me, it's all good."

"Maybe," Brooke said. "But that still leaves their second condition."

"Second condition?"

"Have you heard of Spencer Dean?"

"Sure. He used to flip houses on television. He's also a client."

"Really?" Brooke leaned back, surprised. "He's buying a place in Austin?"

"More than a place," Amanda said. "I've shown him the Drysdale Mansion several times now. I think he's close to making an offer. I hope so. Talk about a delicious commission."

"The Drysdale Mansion?" Brooke's throat had tightened and her pulse had skittered at the mention of the house. And of the only man she'd ever loved. The man with whom she'd shared so many forbidden memories inside those walls.

The man who now despised her.

"What is it?" Amanda asked, peering at Brooke in a way that suggested she saw too much.

Brooke poked at a spicy tuna roll with a chopstick, avoiding Amanda's eyes. "I just always liked that house."

"Hmm." Amanda didn't sound convinced, but also didn't press the point. "At any rate, what does Spencer Dean have to do with your meeting?"

"They want him on the show."

"Really?" Amanda frowned. "He told me he's not in television anymore. Why would he bullshit me?"

"He wasn't," Brooke assured her. "He left his series about a year ago."

For four of the last five years, Spencer had starred in *Spencer's Place*, a house-flipping program that had been as much about Spencer's personality as about the renovations. Brooke had watched only one episode. It hurt too much to see Spencer on screen. Those dark eyes that she'd once believed knew her so well. Those strong, calloused hands that had stroked her skin. His mustache and beard that had tickled her ear as he'd whispered sweet, sexy, decadent things.

He'd held her close and they'd made so many plans, so many promises. She'd loved him fiercely, and she'd believed that he felt the same. A wild, protective love that shone so bright it could cut through any darkness and heal any pain.

And then everything had shattered.

Richie. Her father. And, of course, Brian.

Oh, God, Brian. She fought a shudder of revulsion and

wished that she'd never allowed that vile name into her head.

He was the other reason Brooke hadn't watched Spencer's show. It brought back too many memories of the years when the three of them had been friends. Yes, it hurt to see Spence. But the memories of Brian made her curl up into a useless ball of pain and self-loathing.

"Okay, I get it," Amanda said as she added some wasabi to her soy sauce. "Spencer's show was super popular, and they think he'll bring in the sponsors." Amanda pointed a chopstick at Brooke. "But if he's retired from television, what makes them think he'll do it?"

"The producers told me he still owes them a show. Under his last contract, I mean. So they want him to be on *The Business Plan* with me. They say it's the perfect vehicle."

"Well, then what's the problem? I mean, if he has to do a show to satisfy his contract, why not do this one? And having him can only help your show, right? I'm not seeing the issue."

Brooke had leaned back in her chair, then stared her friend down. "Because if he refuses, then there is no show. They were very clear. No Spencer Dean, no *The Business Plan*. I'm blonde and perky and camera-friendly—"

"They did *not* say that!"

"Pretty much. But they also said I'm no Spencer Dean. I'm not tried and true. I'm not popular. And I'm not getting the show without him."

"I still don't see why you're worried. He owes them a show anyway. Why wouldn't he do the season with you?"

"I can think of a lot of reasons," Brooke admitted. "But the biggest is probably that we used to be engaged."

Chapter Three

DON'T WORRY *about the Spencer part yet. Just lock in* The Fix.

Amanda's parting words played like a mantra through Brooke's head all through her meeting with Jenna. And apparently the mantra worked, because before she knew it, Jenna held out her hand. "The Fix is totally in."

"That's wonderful," Brooke said, hoping her palms weren't sweating with nerves. "You won't regret it."

"I know I won't, and I'm so excited to be working with you. And the show is fabulous. Absolutely perfect for what we're trying to accomplish, and nothing I could have arranged myself. You're pretty much my favorite person right now."

Brooke laughed. "Trust me. The feeling is mutual." And, hopefully, Jenna wouldn't change her mind about Brooke if the whole thing fell through. Which it might. Because Spencer was still a great big question mark. Not that Jenna knew that, because Brooke had taken the coward's way out and told Jenna that the show was exactly the kind of project Spencer Dean was looking for.

It was a flat-out lie, but Brooke needed this opportunity too much to feel any guilt.

"You'll get the green light from the network as soon as Spencer Dean confirms that he's on board?" Jenna asked, as if she'd been reading Brooke's mind. "And you're pretty confident he's in?"

"Are you kidding?" Brooke waved her hand, copying Amanda's dismissive gesture. "I'm already starting prep."

"Great." Jenna pushed back from the table. "Drinks and appetizers are on the house tonight. I hope you stay for a while and enjoy yourself."

"Thanks. I will. Oh, there's Amanda."

Both women waved, then headed over to their mutual friend.

"You two look positively perky. Guess I can add match-making to my list of amazing skills."

"You can," Jenna said. "And because you're so awesome, I'll tell you what I told Brooke—drinks and appetizers on the house tonight."

"And that's why I love you," Amanda said. "Come on, Brooke. Let me introduce you to a Jalapeño Margarita. Trust me, these things are fucking amazing. Are you off?" she added to Jenna. "Want to join?"

"With only about a week before we launch the calendar contest? I'm pretty much on twenty-four seven. Thanks, though. You guys have fun."

As Jenna headed toward the back of the room, Amanda led Brooke to two seats that had opened up at the crowded oak bar.

"Well?" Amanda demanded as soon as they were settled on the tall bar stools. "Didn't I tell you it would be great?"

"Yes, you're amazing and awesome, and I bow to your brilliance."

Amanda's smile broadened. "And that's why I keep you around."

"Speaking of people to keep around, who's that?" Brooke nodded toward the absolutely gorgeous guy now talking with Jenna.

Amanda turned dutifully toward the broad shouldered hunk of awesomeness with the shaved head and the sleeve of tats revealed by his *The Fix on Sixth* T-shirt. "Oh, that's Reece. He's the bar's manager. He's also Jenna's boyfriend."

The latter could have gone unsaid. It was obvious in the way he gently caressed her lower back as she spoke to him. And just as obvious in the way she looked at him, as if any minute he wasn't touching her was one minute too long.

Brooke swallowed a lump in her throat as she glanced away. Once upon a time, she'd felt that way. As if any moment without Spencer was a moment that didn't need to exist. As if she didn't need to have any secrets from him, because their love was perfect and pure, and no matter what demons stepped into their path, they'd conquer them together.

Yeah, she'd been an idiot. A young, foolish, trusting idiot.

Beside her, Amanda lifted her hand and signaled to a tall, lanky bartender with an action hero build and clean-cut dark hair. "Hey, Eric. Can I get two Jalapeño Margaritas?"

"No Cosmo?" Eric asked.

"Cam made a JM for me last night, and it was like an orgasm in my mouth." She smiled at Brooke, who wasn't sure if she should laugh or beg Eric to just give her a beer.

"Seriously. Once you've had a spicy, hot Jalapeño, you're not going back."

"Oh, my God, Amanda. Remind me why we're friends?"

Amanda winked one dark brown eye. "Because all the rest of your friends are boring and tame."

"Fair enough," Brooke said. "Jalapeño me."

"You got it," Eric said. "Anything to eat?"

"Hell, yeah," Amanda said. "Put in an order of Lasagna Rolls for us. Freaking amazing," she added as an aside to Brooke. "Trust me."

"Got it," Eric said, then moved down the bar.

"He's a total hottie," Amanda whispered. "And he's single. Want me to hook you up?"

"Are you kidding? He's what? Twenty-one." An incredibly hot twenty-one, but still.

"He's twenty-five, actually," Amanda said, a little haughtily. "And a very mature twenty-five."

"Oh, really? And do you have personal knowledge of his ... maturity?"

Amanda made a face. "Don't be crass," she said, as Brooke burst out laughing. Amanda talked a good game, but Brooke seriously doubted she saw as much action as her boasting suggested.

"At any rate," Amanda continued, "twenty-five is totally in your range."

"Um, hello? I'm almost thirty."

Amanda flashed her *please, girlfriend* look. "You're twenty-eight."

"Only five months from twenty-nine. And that makes me almost thirty."

"That makes you bad at math."

"Fine. Whatever. But I'm not sleeping with Eric."

"Sorry, what?" the man in question asked as he slid their drinks in front of them.

"Just repeating your name," Brooke said, flashing what she hoped was an innocent smile. "Trying to get everyone's names down since I'll be spending a lot of time here soon."

"Yeah? I saw you with Jenna. You gonna be doing work on the calendar contest?"

"Looks that way."

Eric's eyes caught hers, then held. "Glad to hear it," he said, then turned away to greet another customer.

"My, my, my," Amanda hummed.

"Drop it," Brooke ordered, although she couldn't deny the little tingle of pleasure that came from being noticed by a hot guy. For the most part, she kept herself closed off. She dated, but she didn't do relationships. And sex was always on her terms. Always.

The truth was, she'd lost the ability to trust, to let go. *Lost it?* No, that was bullshit. Trust had been ripped away from her, and though she desperately wanted to get it back, the few times she'd let a guy test her boundaries had been completely disastrous.

Fucking Brian. One betrayal. And her whole world had unraveled. And all she'd wanted to do when the world had spun out from under her was run to Spencer. But he was long gone, an artifact of a life that she'd given up to save him. Except he didn't know any of that. And now he hated her. And she was all alone with her angst and her fear doing her damnedest to build a replacement life. And she was close—so damn close.

But now here came Spencer waltzing back into the thick of it, and Brooke knew damn well how much that was going to hurt.

Fuck.

"Earth to Brooke," Amanda trilled. "Where'd you go? Or is the margarita so amazing that I need to give you a moment alone with it."

"Pretty much," Brooke said, taking another long sip. It really was amazing. The traditional margarita tanginess, but laced with a kick of heat that seemed to do back flips on her tongue.

"Well, don't fade on me again. I want the scoop."

Brooke tilted her head, confused. "What scoop would that be?"

"First off, what happened to the engagement? Why didn't you and Spencer get married? And for that matter, how is it that I didn't know that you and Spencer were a thing?"

Brooke hesitated, not wanting to open old wounds. But it was too late for that. The wounds had opened the moment that Andy and Molly, the network's executives, had given her the ultimatum. Spencer was back, whether she wanted him or not.

And she *did* want him. She'd never stopped. Not really.

But she'd hurt him, and the wounds were too deep to heal. Now, the best that she could hope for was a way to dull the pain so that they could work together. Assuming, of course, that he would even agree.

"From the look on your face, I'm guessing he dumped you?"

"It's complicated," Brooke said, in what had to be the understatement of the year. "My parents never approved of Spencer. His family—well, you've met my dad. It was bad enough that I was dating a guy whose family lived paycheck to paycheck. But toss in the fact that he has a brother in prison because of a gang-related shooting? To say Daddy didn't approve was putting it mildly."

"Probably didn't help that Spencer doesn't hide where he comes from. I watched his show all the time—I mean, real estate, right? And I remember he did one episode where he helped two brothers—former gangbangers—fix up their grandparents' house. Said he wanted to increase awareness and help the guys learn some practical skills."

"I didn't know that," Brooke admitted, although it didn't surprise her. Spencer was a good guy. A solid guy. And her father had simply refused to see that. She smiled ruefully. "I didn't watch the show. Seeing him—it hurt my heart."

Amanda reached over, then pressed her hand over Brooke's. "Your dad did something to end it?"

Brooke nodded, but then immediately shook her head. As tempting as it might be to lay all the blame at her father's feet, she had to take some responsibility.

She wiped away an errant tear. "It was me, too. I—" She cut herself off, her voice choked with a fresh flood of tears. Dammit, she hadn't meant to cry. She drew in a stuttering breath, sniffed, and began again. "I didn't—"

"No," Amanda said in a tone that was uncharacteristically gentle. "It's okay. I didn't mean to bring it all back. And I think I have the general picture. Big, ugly mess with lots and lots of drama."

Despite herself, a bubble of laughter rose, mixing with the knot of tears in her throat and making Brooke hiccup. The painful kind that felt like a fist hitting her heart. "That about sums it up," she said, forcing the words out between hiccups. "And, yeah, drama was the operative word."

"When was this? Before we knew each other, obviously."

Brooke took a sip of her margarita, then waited, her hand on her chest in anticipation of another massive hiccup that didn't come. She drew a tentative breath, then nodded. "It was five years ago. A few weeks before his first show started filming."

"Holy crap. I remember reading about that. Not at the time, but later after his show became popular. I remember there was talk about him being on *The Bachelor* or some similar show. But he said no—like a serious, big ass, *no*—and the tabloids started talking about why he kept such a low profile and hardly ever dated and all that stuff."

She pointed a well-manicured finger at Brooke. "The rumor was that his bride had left him at the altar. That was you?"

Brooke bit her lower lip and nodded, desperate to change the conversation. But, then again, she might as well get used to it. If Spencer agreed to the show—or rather, *when* Spencer agreed to the show—their past would surely be dredged up and splashed all over social media. She'd never understood why, but even the stars of real estate based shows routinely ended up as social media celebrities.

And then it hit her.

She looked up, her gaze locked tight on Amanda's face. "That's what they want, isn't it? They want the drama."

For a moment, Amanda looked baffled. And in that brief, wonderful instant, Brooke let herself believe that she was wrong, and the studio didn't care about her break-up with Spencer and had no interest in playing up their past relationship on camera.

Then she saw the truth in Amanda's eyes. Her friend wasn't baffled by that particular suggestion; she was simply flabbergasted that Brooke was only now figuring it out.

"You honestly didn't know? I mean, it's pretty obvious," Amanda continued in reply to Brooke's shake of the head. "As far as they're concerned, you're the girl who dumped

Spencer Dean. Not an Austin-based remodeling expert. They're casting the woman who can bring fireworks. They don't care about The Fix or even the hot guys in a calendar contest."

"They want drama," Brooke said, feeling both numb and stupid.

"Afraid so. They must think you two will be a ratings magnet." Amanda lifted a shoulder as she took the last sip of her spicy, tangy drink. "That's why if Spencer doesn't agree, your chance at a show is dead in the water."

Chapter Four

BROOKE CLUTCHED her hairbrush as she peered at her reflection in the ladies' room mirror. Sometimes she hated how blunt Amanda was, but couldn't deny it was true. The network had chosen her proposal over all others not because Brooke knew how to breathe life into a rundown restaurant or how to add some pizazz to a dull bar.

No, they wanted her because of a bad break-up. Which meant that the show wasn't going to be about her work at all. It was going to be about her life.

Maybe she should just walk away.

It wasn't as if she had any great desire to be on television. Quite the contrary. If it weren't for the promotional value, she'd be more than happy to live her life well outside of the public eye.

But the show *would* promote her business—that much was a guarantee. After their meeting, one of the producers had texted her rough mock-ups of print ads that would advertise the show. Assuming, of course, that Spencer signed on and the show actually aired. Slick, classy-looking ads that splashed the name of the show in big, bold letters —and the show shared a name with her business.

Not only that, but the ads also included her website and contact information, in equally eye-catching fonts.

It was as if the execs had known she might get cold feet and had wanted to make sure she was all in.

Well, it worked.

She wasn't going to back off the show. Not even now that Amanda had opened her eyes.

But as for *why* she was sticking...

Well, the horrible truth was she wasn't sure if that was because she couldn't bear to turn her back on any possible promotion for her business ... or because of Spencer.

She missed him.

Dear God, she missed him.

Those months surrounding their wedding had felt like a goddamn Greek tragedy. At the time, she'd been so sure she'd done the right thing. Protecting his family. His show. She'd sacrificed everything for him, then held the secret close because he couldn't know. Hell, he still didn't know what she'd done.

She'd believed she could move on with her life. That there would be another man who could make her feel the way that Spence had. And maybe there was. Maybe that mystical guy was out there in the world somewhere. But if so, she hadn't found him yet.

But even though some secret part deep inside her wanted to see him again, she was certain the feeling wouldn't be mutual. She wasn't naive enough to believe that Spencer had forgiven her. Not for walking away on their wedding day. And certainly not for what he'd perceived as betrayal.

No doubt about it—their meeting was going to bruise her heart all over again.

But if it launched her business to a new level, it would be worth it.

She needed to keep repeating that to herself. Over and over and over.

She shoved her brush back into her purse, then started for the ladies' room exit, only to jump back when someone pushed the door open with so much force it slammed back against the wall. Two women stumbled in, laughing uncontrollably.

"The floor is moving," the dark-haired one said. She was looking down at the completely motionless floor, but then she lifted her head to glare at her companion. "I totally blame you," she said at the same time that Brooke gasped.

"Shelby?" Brooke said, peering at the woman. It couldn't be. Brooke's accountant was about the most straight-laced, calm, and introverted person Brooke had ever met. And although theirs was a mostly professional relationship, Brooke and Shel had gone out socially a couple of times—and Shelby had never ordered anything stronger than Perrier with lime.

So this laughing, stumbling, well-on-her-way-to-wasted woman couldn't possibly be Shelby Drake, CPA.

Except it was.

Shelby blinked owlishly behind aqua-framed glasses. Then her eyes widened in time with a spreading grin. "Brooke Hamlin!" She threw out her arms and enveloped her in a hug. "Isn't this the best party?"

"Um, yeah?"

Brooke glanced up at Shelby's companion, a tall

woman with a mass of unkempt curls and an expression that could only be described as amused. "Hannah," she said, thrusting out her hand. "Also known as Shelby's babysitter."

"Like hell," Shel said, then clasped a hand over her mouth. "Oh, dear." She stumbled toward the single, empty stall and locked the door behind her.

Brooke looked between the closed stall door and Hannah. "So, ah, was there an alien invasion that didn't make the news? Because Shelby's been my family's accountant for years, and that's not Shelby."

Hannah laughed. "Isn't it awesome? We're here for a friend's bachelorette party, and I told Shel she had to let her hair down."

"You're evil," Shel said from the stall.

"But you love me," Hannah called back. She tilted her head as she studied Brooke, her eyes a little foggy. She'd clearly been drinking, too. She just had a much higher tolerance than Shelby. Or else she'd drunk half as much. "Have we met?"

"I don't think so." Brooke was sure she'd remember the woman with her wild hair and piercing blue eyes.

"Damn, you look so familiar, but I can't—*wait*. Are you Judge Hamlin's daughter?"

Brooke stiffened. "Yeah. That's my dad." Formerly a powerful attorney, her father had recently run for a District Court seat. He won, of course. With the exception of her career choice, her father always got what he wanted.

"I'm a lawyer, and I've worked with your dad a couple of times. I think I remember your picture from his office. Or maybe from a fundraiser for his campaign?"

"Maybe," Brooke said, though she didn't remember

Hannah at all. But they didn't press the connection because Shel emerged from the stall, then grinned.

"I feel better," she said, then used one of the little cups to squirt out some complimentary mouthwash. She swished and spit, then smiled ruefully at Brooke, who hid her amused grin behind a fake cough.

"Want to join us for a drink?" Hannah asked.

"No, thanks. I need to get going." She'd taken approximately a billion photos of the interior of The Fix, and she wanted to work through her plans for the renovation, this time thinking about it in terms of which design elements to focus on during each of the six episodes.

"You sure?" Shelby pulled her into a one-armed hug. "Because it's really so awesome to see you."

"You, too," Brooke said, catching Hannah's eye and laughing. "Come on. I'll walk out with you, at least."

"We should get back," Hannah said. "That cute bartender said he was making us pitchers of Pinot Punch, and those bitches will snarf it all down if we don't hurry back. Our friends are a cut-throat group," she said to Brooke, her eyes dancing.

Brooke tagged along as they headed back into the main bar area. There was no question where they were headed —straight toward the gaggle of laughing, drinking girls taking up the three tables in the front alcove. It was a primo spot, with the tables tucked in between a massive Austin wall mural and the floor-to-ceiling windows that looked out over the hustle and bustle of Sixth Street.

The girls were talking among themselves, their attention mostly on the pretty blonde in the tacky tiara with BRIDE spelled out in fake gemstones. But a few of the women were looking back at the polished wooden bar, where several guys were seated on stools—and were looking right back at them.

"He's still there," Shelby whispered, bumping into Brooke as she reached for Hannah. "Do you think he's— oh, shit. He's looking this way."

"Just go talk to him," Hannah urged. "He's obviously noticed you. And you have *so* noticed him."

"Who?" Brooke asked. She wasn't part of the group, and she didn't even really know Shelby. But she couldn't contain her curiosity.

"Him," Hannah said. She started to lift a finger, but Shelby clutched her hand, holding it down.

"Don't point! The cute guy right there, with the short hair and the *The best mornings have Wood* T-shirt. Oh my God," she hissed at Brooke. "Why are you waving at him?"

"He's a friend," Brooke explained. "His name's Nolan Wood. And the tacky shirt is the name of his morning show. *Mornings With Wood.* He does crazy ass commentary for one of the local radio stations."

"You know him?" From the awe in Shelby's voice, you'd think Brooke had announced that he was royalty.

"Casually. He used to date a friend."

"Oh."

"He's single now," Brooke said, hearing the disappoint- ment in Shel's voice. "I think."

"Just *go*," Hannah said, then turned to Brooke. "I keep telling her to go introduce herself and say hi."

"I can introduce you. His show is all about being snarky and crass and chatty between songs during morning drive time. I wanted to run something by him." Free publicity, actually, but she didn't need to get into that with the girls.

"Yes," Hannah said. "Perfect. Go."

"But—"

"*Go.*"

"We'll all go," Brooke said. It felt very junior high, but what the hell? She could chat with Nolan about giving her show and The Fix a few shout-outs, and she could introduce him to her normally very shy and reserved accountant. Seriously, was this *really* Shelby Drake?

They weaved their way across most of the bar, but right as Brooke reached Nolan, she realized that she'd lost both Shelby and Hannah. She glanced over her shoulder to see Shel hanging back and Hannah looking exasperated. Brooke rolled her eyes, amused but not surprised. Somehow she didn't think that flirting with guys was a normal thing for Shelby. And neither, for that matter, was getting drunk.

At least she looked like she was having a good time.

"I can't believe you were going to walk right over to him," Shelby said once Brooke had abandoned her mission and navigated her way back. The band that had been on a break was about to start a new set, and the crowd around the bar and the stage was getting thicker.

"Well, I thought I was going with you," Brooke said. "Didn't y'all say he noticed you earlier? Besides, he doesn't bite."

"At least not unless you ask him to," Hannah quipped, making Shelby blush.

"I really can't," Shelby said. "I mean isn't it..." She trailed off with a shake of her head. "I'm not usually so bold. Are you?" She turned to Brooke, whose eyes went wide.

"Me?"

"Yeah. Would you ever throw caution to the wind like that?"

Brooke thought of Spencer. Of the way she'd met him in a dark street beside a useless car. He'd pulled up on that fabulous motorcycle, all tats and beard and leather, and everything she'd ever been taught had urged her to run like hell.

But she'd seen something in his eyes, and so she'd stayed. And for better or worse, her life had never been the same.

"I have," she whispered. "I did."

"Oh." Shelby and Hannah exchanged glances. "What happened?"

Brooke forced a smile and blinked back the tears that threatened. "I fell in love," she said, then felt the tug of a bittersweet smile as the lump of unshed tears tightened in her chest.

"Careful," Hannah said lightly, obviously not noticing the shift in Brooke's mood. "You might scare her off."

Brooke thought about how things turned out for her. Maybe that would be a good thing.

But, no. Shelby deserved her shot, too.

"Go talk to him," she urged, then started to raise her hand to catch Nolan's attention. But at that moment, a group of men at the bar moved away—and there *he* stood in the gap.

Spencer.

He leaned against the polished bar, a highball glass in his hand. Glenmorangie, neat. She didn't need to taste the liquor to know, because she knew the man. He didn't do cocktails, just Scotch or beer. And Glenmorangie was his favorite label.

From where she stood, she could see his profile, and she

was certain that he hadn't noticed her. He'd let his beard grow out a little, so that it looked more like it had the first time they'd met, and she had to admit she liked it. Once they'd started dating, it had been neatly trimmed, and she'd always felt like he was playing a role. Hell, maybe he was. Trying to be the clean-cut, middle class guy that her father would approve of.

Now, the beard was a little unkempt. A little wild. And for one fleeting moment, she wanted to feel those dark whiskers on her cheeks again. Her lips. Her thighs.

He cocked his head, as if he'd heard someone call him. As if, she thought, he'd picked up on all the decadent images running wild through her head.

She froze, and Hannah looked back at her curiously.

"I—I forgot something in the ladies' room. Y'all go on ahead. Nolan's a really nice guy. Just introduce yourself."

"What—"

But Brooke turned away, cutting off Shelby's words, because Spencer had turned toward them, and like a coward, Brooke was going to bolt.

She had no idea if he'd seen her, and she wasn't going to hang around to find out. She knew she couldn't put off talking to him forever—especially if they were doing a show together—but she needed time to prepare. And one minute wasn't nearly enough.

She slipped back into the hallway that led to the restrooms and office space. She assumed there would be an emergency exit down there, but after she passed the closed office door and turned the corner, she realized the space was little more than an alcove with some shelving for paper supplies. Napkins, paper towels, toilet paper, rolls of receipts. *Damn.*

The exit to the alley must have been the other direction, back toward the kitchen.

She turned, took one step, then squealed as Spencer pushed her back into the dark corner, his palm firm on her shoulder.

"Brooke," he murmured in that familiar, rough voice. "I think it's time we had a little talk."

Chapter Five

"WHAT THE HELL, BROOKE?" His voice rolled over her like salted caramel, rough and sweet at the same time. "Was it not enough that you yanked my heart out? Then stomped on every goddamn thing I thought was true and real and right? Now you have to come back so that you can rip open the scars? I mean, Christ. You've stayed away from me for five goddamn years. Why the hell are you back in my life now?"

She tensed, her insides coiled like a spring about to snap. She told herself she wasn't scared, but that was a lie. She was terrified. She just didn't know if she was afraid of Spencer—or of her own reaction to him. Trepidation, yes. But underscored with genuine desire.

In other words, she was screwed.

"Let go of me." The words were low and forceful, and she congratulated herself on her voice not shaking.

His brown eyes hardened, but he complied—and she immediately regretted the demand. He wasn't touching her now, true. But both his hands were on the wall on either side of her, effectively caging her in and putting his entire body in extreme proximity to hers.

Years ago, the wild pounding of her heart and the lightness in her head would have been evidence of excitement. Right now, though, it was fear.

Not that she thought Spence would hurt her—she didn't. But she couldn't breathe like that, with him trapping her, stealing away what little control she had over the situation. Not anymore. Not after what happened.

"Back off." She'd intended the words as a demand, but they sounded choked and weak. She lifted her chin and straightened her spine. Hadn't her father always told her that *looking* in control was almost the same as *being* in control?

He didn't move. For that matter, he didn't say a word.

"I mean it," she said, feeling stronger. "If you want to talk, then call me, and we can meet for coffee. You don't have to manhandle me." Brooke forced her voice to stay steady, and she hoped he couldn't hear the pounding rhythm of her heart. He was close—so close she could taste the whisky on his breath. "Or is that the way you roll now? Intimidating women in dark corners?"

Still, he said nothing. But he kept his eyes on her face, studying her intently as if she was a problem he had to solve. Which, frankly, she pretty much was.

The silence lingered, thick and heavy, until she couldn't stand it any longer. "Spencer. Please."

She didn't know what he heard in her voice. But he took two steps back, his arms falling away, freeing her.

For a moment, his expression seemed gentle. Almost understanding. And she allowed herself to listen to the small, pitiful voice that said he would forgive her. That she'd done the right thing five years ago, and eventually the universe would correct itself.

Brooke knew there was no chance for a future with Spencer—she'd had no illusions when she walked away, and she'd made her peace with that. But it hurt more than she'd ever believed possible to know that the man who'd once loved her so tenderly, now despised her beyond all measure. Even if that hate was inevitable.

"Tell me about this show." The words—barked out like a military order—surprised her, and she responded without thinking.

"I have a remodeling business. Here. In Austin, I mean. And there was a call for proposals. I submitted, and—"

"And you thought you'd toss me into the mix?"

"The hell I did," she snapped.

He tilted his head to the side, nodding slowly. "That's exactly what you did. Tossed me into the mix. Made sure *your* show has *my* name. And figured I'd prostrate myself because I owe the network one more goddamn show."

"Like I said, it wasn't my idea." She set her jaw, annoyed that he'd think for a moment that she manufactured that nonsense.

He stepped closer, still not touching her, but so close she could feel his breath on her hair. "But you didn't say no, did you?"

She didn't answer; what would be the point? Obviously, she hadn't protested. If she had, they wouldn't be standing here.

He nodded, his tight expression suggesting that he'd solved some daunting puzzle. "I'll do your show, Angel—"

"Don't call me that." *Not that way. Not like a curse when it used to be an endearment.*

His eyes narrowed, the change almost undetectable,

but she saw it. For a moment, she even thought she saw compassion in his eyes. Then they went cold and hard, and he nodded. One quick, tight jerk of his head.

"I'll do your show, *Brooke*," he said. "But I'll do it on my terms."

"Your terms." She didn't want to react, but she couldn't help but swallow. "Okay. I'll bite. What exactly do you want?"

Once again, his hand went to the wall, but this time it was so he could lean in until his mouth was kissing-close to her ear. "You," he said. And, damn her, she felt the word reverberate through her, like a hot wire touching every part of her and teasing her with a fire she was no longer allowed to touch. For one precious moment, hope filled her. But then she saw the hardness in his eyes, and the hope slithered away, dark and lost and lonely. "I want you at my mercy."

"I—I don't understand."

"It's simple, baby. You want me on your show, then we're together again. Completely. Totally."

He pushed back, but let the hand that was on the wall trail down her arm, from her shoulder to her hand. She stood frozen, forcing herself not to flinch, to cry, to run.

What horrible kind of game was he playing?

She wanted to ask—hell, she wanted to shout. But she was afraid to speak, even though he was looking at her as if expecting her to say something.

When she didn't, the corner of his mouth curled up a little. And she wasn't sure if she'd scored a point ... or walked right into his hands.

"I want you to remember what it felt like. I want you to relive how you exploded in my arms. I want you to beg for me, baby. And when the show wraps, this time it'll be me who walks away."

She wanted to shout at him. To pound her fists on his chest and tell him that this wasn't fair. She'd had no choice. No choice at all. Because her choices had been ripped away from her, leaving the unhealed wounds that he was now poking.

She didn't shout. She didn't cry. She simply stood there, taking in his pain and his anger, telling herself that she could stand it because she had to.

"What kind of game were you playing, Brooke? Was the plan to use me to learn the business? To get your rocks off? Or was that just a side benefit? What made you walk? Was I not dark enough for you? Not bad enough to keep Daddy pissed off?"

She didn't realize she'd slapped him until she felt the sting of impact against her palm. "I knew you were rough, but I never thought you were cruel."

He rubbed his cheek. "Cruel? Baby, you invented the word."

"You son-of-a-bitch. You have no idea what—*dammit.*" She clamped her mouth shut, determined not to speak.

"You know my terms. Take them or leave them."

She opened her mouth to reply, but he pressed a finger to her lips. "Molly and Andy are in LA. They'll be back on Wednesday with the contracts. The meeting's at eleven. If you show up—if you agree to the deal—that means you agree to my terms, too. All my terms."

He brushed a finger over her lower lip. "I want to be clear before you decide. We do this, and you're mine. Any time I want, any way I want. Complete control. I'll punish you, baby. Believe me. But I'll also bring you so much plea-sure that you'll beg me not to stop. Not to ever stop. But

41

that's the kicker, my pretty little angel. Because in the end, I will stop. I will walk away. And this time, you'll be the one left wanting me."

He trailed the finger down from her lower lip, then along her neck to stroke her collarbone before dropping lower to brush, ever so lightly, over her nipple. And then, to her mortification, she drew in a breath that shuddered with desire.

He didn't move, but she saw the realization in his eyes. And when his lips quirked into a grin, she knew that she'd lost this round.

"You want your show?" he said. "Well, I want revenge."

And then he turned and left the alcove, disappearing into the dark as Brooke's knees gave out, and she sank to the floor ... and into her memories.

Chapter Six

Five years ago

"YOU'RE CRAZY," Spencer said, laughing as he pulled Brooke into his lap. "You know that right?"

She snuggled close, breathing in the scent of sawdust and turpentine. "Just because I think we should drive away after the wedding on your bike instead of a limo? That doesn't make me crazy. Just crazy for you."

She lifted her head long enough to kiss his lower lip, right above his beard, then relaxed as his arms tightened around her.

"Well, then we're equal. Because I'm nuts about you, too." Humor and love laced his voice, and she smiled to herself, happy to hear that tone of joy. These last few days had been so damn hard for him. Hell, for all of them.

Honestly, the news was so tragic—so heartbreaking— that she'd even suggested postponing the wedding. But he wouldn't hear of it. "Postponing the wedding wouldn't change anything. And besides, I can't give you the chance to find someone better, can I?"

His tone was joking, but the words made her wince. Because even though she loved him with a ferocity that sometimes scared her, she knew that he secretly feared that she'd come to her senses, realize her parents were right, and find a man with an MD and a trust fund to marry.

As if.

Brooke might only be twenty-three, but she knew who she wanted. And that was Spencer. And she didn't give a flying fuck what her parents thought of him or his family.

Spencer had never hidden his background from her. He'd told her over and over that he knew her family would disapprove, and he wanted her to go into the relationship with eyes open. And because he'd wanted her from the first moment he saw her, he'd told her his story on the night they'd met.

It had been getting on toward midnight almost two years ago when he'd pulled up on his bike and helped her change a tire. Well, *help* wasn't entirely accurate, as she'd been doing nothing other than searching her purse for her AAA car so that she could call for assistance. But assistance had materialized in the form of a dark man with an unkempt beard, a leather jacket, and the kind of tight jeans that had made her breath catch in her throat.

He'd changed the tire in record time, then asked if he could buy her a beer. She'd never known for sure what made her say yes, but she thought it was something in his eyes. The flecks of gold in the brown that looked like starlight and seemed to promise her the universe. As if he held the power to lay the world at her feet.

Her *yes* had been barely audible, but it had been enough. And she'd followed him in her car to a divey joint tucked away in a section of East Austin into which she'd never ventured.

They'd played pool, drank beer, and swapped life stories. And he'd made no bones about the fact that he'd grown up piss-poor in one of the roughest neighborhoods in East Austin. Or that his brother was on death row. "I want you to know," he'd said. And she'd desperately wanted to hear.

"My dad—Billy—was as white trash as they come, and in his teens and twenties, his gang was his family." But then Billy met Carina, the woman who would become Spencer's mom, and he'd sworn to clean up his act. He managed to extricate himself from gang life and made a decent living doing construction work. They got married, had Richie, and then seven years later, Spencer came along.

But Carina died when Spencer was four. Complications from a third pregnancy, and neither mother nor child made it.

"I only remember bits and pieces, but my dad pretty much spun out. And that's when Richie stepped in to be the man of the house. All of eleven, and he was supporting all of us."

"That's not possible."

"Yeah," Spence had said. "It is. He just had to find another kind of family."

"A gang."

"The Crimson Eights. Fingers in drugs, guns, probably human trafficking, though I don't know for sure. Heard of them?"

She'd shook her head. "I don't think so."

"You said you live in Westlake, right?"

She felt embarrassed to admit that she came from such a well-off Austin neighborhood, but she gave a little nod. "So?"

"I'm not surprised you haven't heard. Not much in the way of grit is reported in that area."

"You talk like you know it."

"I went to Trinity," he'd said, then laughed as her eyes went wide at the reference to the exclusive private school. "Don't worry. No gang dollars financed my education. I was there from middle school through my sophomore year. Their scholarship program. It's all about community outreach. My brother really pushed my dad to get me in, and so Dad pretty much hounded the committee until they relented."

"That's great."

He nodded. "Yeah. My dad got his shit back together once he realized what Richie was doing to keep food on our table. And he made it his mission to make sure I didn't get sucked into the gang life. Not hard, because Richie didn't want me in it either."

"But Richie stayed in?"

"He stayed in," Spencer had acknowledged. "Despite my dad's pushing and prodding and fighting." He exhaled. "And that choice cost Richie everything."

The death penalty.

It had cost Spencer, too. He'd dropped out school after Richie's arrest. "I went off the rails," he'd told her. "I was angry at the world. At life. At fucking everything. Was lucky I didn't get tossed into foster care or into a juvie center. Or, hell, tried as an adult. You'd think I'd know better after Richie, but it was like I was trying to be like him. Basically, I was a fucking mess."

"But you got it together," she'd said, and he'd nodded. "I put all my energy into working with my hands. Carpentry. Bricklaying. Roofing. Framing. Electrical work. If I didn't already know it, I learned it."

Now, safe in Spencer's arms on the couch, she thought about the man she'd met only once behind a piece of Plexiglass. A man who'd been living in a cell for ten years by then. They'd spoken to each other across an old-fashioned handset, and Spencer had introduced her as his bride-to-be.

Richie's face had bloomed with the news. "You're doing good, little brother. Don't fuck it up."

Spencer had laughed and kissed her. "Never happen."

There'd been hope in the air that day. Richie's lawyers were arguing one more appeal in the morning. With luck, Richie would walk. At the very least, the family was hopeful that he'd be transferred off Death Row.

Brooke shuddered, the pain of the memory washing over her. That hadn't happened.

"You okay?"

"Only a chill," she lied, pulling the soft throw over them both. "I'm perfect."

He chuckled. "Yeah," he said. "You are."

She turned in his arms, then pressed her palm against his cheek. "Are you okay?"

For a moment, she thought he'd lie and tell her that he was fine. That he could handle it. But then he blinked, and she saw the tears in his eyes, and when he spoke, his voice was rough and raw, full of anger and pain and futility.

"I can't believe they're really going to do it. Three more months and then my brother will be gone."

Tears spilled down her own cheeks. "I know. I wish— God, I would give anything to change it. To make it better for him. For you."

They'd learned only yesterday—two days before the wedding—that the last of Richie's appeals had been denied, and his execution date had been set. And Brooke had never felt more helpless than she had when she saw Spencer take the phone call, then collapse into a chair, as if every ounce of strength had left his body.

"You do, Angel," he said as he stroked her hair, her cheek. "Don't you know that you make everything better?"

"Spencer." Emotion overwhelmed her, so intense that she almost couldn't breathe. She'd never in her life felt the way she did in his arms. Cherished. Loved. Beautiful. With Spencer, she believed that everything was possible. That she could follow the life she craved and not the one her parents had planned for her. That she could actually make it work. And it tore at her heart that they both had to face Richie's execution—such harsh evidence that even in the arms of perfection, the world could go horribly, ridiculously wrong.

"Come here," he demanded, though he didn't give her time to respond. Instead, he buried his fingers in her hair at the nape and pulled her down to him. He took her mouth in a long, slow kiss. A kiss that tasted like sunshine and promised the world. A strong, magical kiss that had the power to push them through the pain of Richie's pending execution to the future of a life together.

A kiss that built in passion as they moved against each other, both craving the release. The connection.

She shifted so that she was straddling him. She wore a pair of his old sweatpants, cut off to make shorts, with nothing else underneath. Now, the soft material bunched up her legs so that her bare ass and legs rubbed against his jeans in a deliciously enticing way.

With Spencer, need always hovered close to the surface, and it rose now, the sweetness of that initial kiss giving way to a wild abandon, more intense and desperate today because of all they wanted to forget—Richie's execution, her family's disapproval, the frustration of a world they couldn't control.

But this—the wildness between them—was something they could claim and control and celebrate.

"I need you." Spencer's growl cut through her, his tone affecting her as intimately as a caress.

"You have me." Her voice came out raspy with need. "Please, Spencer. I—"

"Yes. God, yes." He captured her in a kiss again, and this time, his free hand slid under her tank top, his fingers teasing her bare breast and sending ripples of electricity rolling through her body.

Shamelessly, she ground against his pelvis, still tightly clad in denim. He was hard, his erection straining, and, dammit, she didn't want to wait. With her mouth, she nipped at his lower lip, and as she did, she used her fingers to fumble open the button on his jeans and carefully lower his zipper.

"Christ," he whispered when she reached in to free him from his boxers. "If you want to go slow, I think I just might die."

"Fast," she agreed as his fingers slid up her thigh, then under the fleece of her shorts. She was desperately wet, and he teased her with his fingertip, playing with her clit and making her breath come in gasps.

"Please," she begged. "I want you inside me."

He complied, thrusting a finger into her, which she rode shamelessly, all the while telling him that his finger wasn't what she had in mind.

"Then show me," he teased, and she reached to untie the drawstring of her shorts. His hand stilled hers. "No," he said, then tugged the crotch aside. "Like this."

The words were like an order, and she obeyed willingly,

rubbing against his cock until the head was at her core, then slowly—so deliciously, painfully slowly—easing him inside. She wanted to ride him slow, to make it last for both of them, but that was out of the question.

Her body was demanding hard and fast—and so was Spencer. He had his hands on her hips, and with each of her thrusts, he drew her down hard, her tender flesh rubbing against the denim he still wore as his length filled her, the sensations inside and against her clit sending her spiraling higher and higher.

"I can't wait," he said, and she cried out that she couldn't either.

She came wildly, violently, her body breaking apart in the most wondrous way, and then slowly and sweetly coming back together in his arms before drifting away on a sea of contentment.

She must have fallen asleep, because the next thing she knew was that she was alone.

"Spencer?" Her voice came out low, groggy, and she pushed herself up on her elbows as she searched the dark room for him.

A sliver of light crept out from around the bathroom door, which had been left cracked slightly. Immediately, a wave of relief washed over her, and only then did she realize how on edge she'd been upon waking without him.

"Silly," she whispered, intending to roll over and go to sleep, but then she heard him. The sobs coming from the bathroom. The anguish of losing a man who'd been like a father to him for so much of his childhood. And the anguish of losing his father, too. Not to death, but to dementia, the victim of a stroke that had knocked the old man down the day Richie's first appeal had been denied.

For a moment, she considered going to him. But she

stayed in bed, the sheet pulled tight around her and her eyes shut tight as she prayed for a way to save Richie. And by saving him, also saving the man she loved.

———

BROOKE HAD MADE peace with the fact that her parents weren't coming to the wedding. Her mother had avoided the real issue, saying that she was on call all week at the hospital and couldn't get away. A ridiculous excuse since the wedding was being held at a friend's house in Central Austin, a short drive from the hospital where Brooke's mother was on staff.

Her father hadn't bothered trying to wrap his absence in a bullshit excuse. He'd simply said that she was a spoiled little fool who didn't appreciate everything he did for her. And that if she was going to marry a man who came from *that* kind of family, then she was on her own.

She'd been okay with that, though it hurt to know that her parents were so quick to cut themselves off from the little girl they'd always claimed to love so fiercely.

Still, she had no illusions about her father. Randall Hamlin saw the world in black and white, not shades of gray. And that was a perspective that had fueled every trial he'd ever won—and so far, that was each and every one of them.

So she'd been unprepared when he arrived at her apartment the night before the wedding.

"You're still determined to go through with this charade, I assume?"

"Daddy, I love you. But I'm done. If you came to try to talk me out of the wedding, then just go away. I have some girlfriends coming over in couple of hours, and we're going to celebrate by drinking wine and watching chick flicks. I really don't need you in my head. Okay?"

She started to close the door, but he stepped over the threshold, a hand thrust out to keep the door open. "That's not why I came. Please, baby girl. Hear me out."

She almost insisted he leave, but it had been so long since he'd used that endearment that her defenses went down. Besides, no matter what else he might be, he was her father. And some desperate, needy part of her wanted to fix things between them.

"Ten minutes," she said, opening the door fully to allow him to enter.

He stepped inside, and before she even had time to offer him a drink, he spoke. "I've been in touch with the governor. I say the word, and he's prepared to grant clemency to Richard Dean."

All of the breath left her body, and she was glad she hadn't reached for her glass of wine. "What do you mean? You can get him released?"

"No. Not that. But I can get his sentence reduced. The death penalty removed. His sentence commuted to life in prison. And with the possibility of parole."

"I see." She licked her lips, her heart pounding so hard she was having a difficult time thinking. "This is—Daddy, this is incredible." She reached for her phone. "I need to call Spencer. He'll be—"

"No."

The word came out with the force of a demand, and she froze, cold terror creeping up her spine.

"You know that I'm close with the governor. And I'll tell you right now that I've already spoken to him about this. I say the word, and he'll take action."

"And you'll say the word when?"

"When you break off this wedding. When you walk away from that man."

She closed her eyes, knowing in that moment how it felt to hate someone you'd once loved. "That's horrible."

"Is it?"

"You're playing with a man's life, and you're making me a pawn in some goddamn medieval game."

"He already chose his path. He drove that car. He was involved in a murder."

"He wasn't," she protested. "He thought he was driving his friend to a convenience store. He had no idea the other guy was going to rob the place, much less kill the clerk."

"He was a participant. And he had a gun."

"Because he always had a gun. It was holstered under his jacket, but he was outside in the parking lot, and—"

"Felony murder," her father said coldly. "He drove the car."

"Wrong time, wrong place," she retorted.

"Perhaps. And perhaps that's why I'm making this offer."

"Contingent on me walking away from the man I love?" This was a nightmare. An epic, horrible nightmare. "You're going to let a man die—"

"The law is clear." Her father's voice was cold. "And so is my conscience."

"Daddy." She heard the plea in her voice and hated it. But she'd get down on her knees and beg if that would convince him.

But there was no convincing him.

"You walk away. You don't tell him why—I won't risk the governor's reputation being tarnished. Or mine, for that matter. You walk, Brooke. And you don't look back."

He left without another word, leaving her alone to

make her choice.

She canceled the girls' night, then spent the longest night of her life trying to decide what to do. A marriage balanced against the weight of the life of a man.

She was still awake when the sun rose, and she numbly dressed to go to her friend's house for the wedding. It wasn't meant to be fancy, and she held her simple white dress over her arm, still not sure what she was going to do.

It wasn't until she saw Brian, Spencer's best friend from Trinity, that everything became clear.

"Hey, gorgeous," he called as she walked down the gravel drive to the guest house where the wedding would be held. She turned, recognizing his voice, but not finding the speaker. Then she saw Brian sitting in the gazebo drinking a beer. She cut over to him and offered him a smile that she hoped looked genuine. Despite it being her wedding day, she wasn't in much of a mood to smile.

He lifted his beer in greeting and offered her a dazzling white grin. With his Robert Redford eyes, blond frat boy looks, and trust fund attitude, Brian hardly seemed like the kind of guy to claim Spencer as a friend. But the two had met on Spence's first day at Trinity and had struck up a solid friendship.

Although they'd taken different paths—Spence dropping out, Brian on the fast track to an MBA—they still saw each other regularly for beer and football and shooting the shit. Often enough, in fact, that Brooke had come to know Brian well, and for the most part, she liked him.

Of course, there'd been a few awkward moments. Brian made no secret that he was attracted to her. And although she was totally devoted to Spencer, she had to admit that he was easy on the eyes. In a world without Spence, she might have willingly caught one of his passes.

But in the world as it was, he was just another pretty piece of scenery on the fringes of her life.

"Is he getting ready?" she asked Brian, who nodded.

"Rough night. He kept talking about how if things were different, Richie would be his best man. Not that he begrudges me the job, but—"

"Yeah. I know."

"You okay?" Brian peered at her.

"Of course. Just not enough sleep. Typical for a bride, right?"

"Mmm." He studied her a moment longer, his frown deepening. "You're not upset about the honeymoon, are you? Or the lack of a honeymoon."

"Are you kidding?" For over a year, Spencer had been pulling strings to land a network real estate flipping program. He'd finally—*finally*—got a contract with The Design and Destination Channel for a show called *Spencer's Place*. The producers had even committed to an unprecedented five-season run. But the kicker was that the producers wanted to start filming right away, and for that to happen, Spencer and Brooke had to cancel their honeymoon.

"We can take a trip anytime," Brooke said honestly. "This opportunity is way too important."

"I thought that's how you felt. But I wanted to make sure. You look a little off."

She forced a grin. "Exactly what a bride wants to hear."

"Wanna tell me?"

She sighed. Since Brian had a thing for her, she generally tried to keep her distance simply because she didn't want him to feel awkward when his interest wasn't returned.

So normally, she would have brushed off his comment, not wanting to get too down in the weeds with him. But today, with her heart hurting and her head confused, she accepted the offer to unburden herself, at least a little. "It's Richie," she said. "I feel so bad about Richie."

"Yeah, it's pretty much killing Spencer. And it's only gonna get worse."

"What do you mean?"

"It's a total fluke, but there's nothing he can do about it. Except Spencer says he can't handle it, and the network says that they can't reschedule. So they're at an impasse. I think Spencer's afraid they're going to throw up their hands and pull the plug."

Alarm bells clanged in her head. "Brian. What are you talking about?"

"The first day of filming. It's the day of Richie's execution."

She shuddered, then closed her eyes, opening them only when she felt Brian take her hand. "He's refusing to show up for filming, isn't he?" She knew the answer. He'd never abandon Richie, and certainly not at the end.

Brian squeezed her hand, and she clung to him, craving comfort.

"Those bastards," she said. "They can't bump it one fucking day?"

"You need to tell him, Brooke," Brian said. "Tell him that Richie wouldn't want him to lose this chance."

She couldn't tell him that. He'd never listen, and she didn't believe it, anyway.

But there was still something she could do. A way to make it better. To save Richie, and to save the show.

And all it would cost was her happiness. And Spencer's.

Chapter Seven

THE FEEL and scent of Spencer stayed with Brooke for days. The way he'd pressed her into that alcove in The Fix. The way his skin had felt against hers. The roughness in his voice. The low, ominous promise of retribution.

And though she tried to concentrate on her work and on her business, it was Spencer—always Spencer—who filled her thoughts.

Him, and the demand he was making. Or, more accurately, the threat.

She hugged herself, replaying the scene in her head. "The meeting's in a couple of hours, and I still honestly don't know what to do," she told Amanda. "He hates me."

"Well, you did leave him at the altar. That's not exactly a recipe for lasting devotion."

Brooke pressed her fingertips to her temples. "Thanks for your insight." They were in Amanda's downtown condo having breakfast on her balcony that overlooked Lady Bird Lake, which wasn't really a lake at all, but a river that ran through downtown Austin. "How can I work with a man who hates me?"

Brooke hadn't told Amanda about Spencer's very specific—very intense—demand. All she'd said was that Spencer had cornered her in The Fix and made it very clear that he didn't appreciate being strong-armed into the show, and that he intended to take out his displeasure on Brooke.

"Professional actors work together all the time, and some of them hate each other," Amanda pointed out. "And you said you walked because of cold feet, right? Have you explained that to him? I mean, it's not ideal, but at least it's understandable."

That had been the story she'd told Spencer on that horrible day. That it was all happening so fast, and that they needed time apart, to think and to grow. She'd thought she could outsmart her father that way. That she and Spencer could put the brakes on. And then, once Richie was safe and there was no going back, she'd explain the deception to Spencer. They'd get back together, and her father would be shit out of luck.

Needless to say, it hadn't worked out that way. Her father knew her well, and he'd told her flat out that if she tried to backdoor the wedding by reconciling with Spencer after the governor granted clemency, then he, her father, would leak Spencer's juvenile record, his gang affiliations, and any other dirt that Mr. Hamlin could dig up on Spencer.

"And then see how that precious show of his fares. No little girl of mine is getting involved with scum. And that's the way it's going to be."

He'd played her like a puppet, and she'd danced for him. Just like she'd done her whole life. And in the end, she'd walked away from the man she'd loved, her only consolation being that she'd saved his brother.

After the wedding was cancelled, she'd gone to Dallas for medical school. Not because she wanted to, but because her father had insisted. And she didn't argue because Spencer wasn't there to give her strength.

She'd been alone. So damnably, horribly alone.

She'd been twenty-three, but she'd felt so much younger. Lost and scared. Lonely and desperate. And angry. Dear God, she'd been furious. With herself. With her father. With the whole goddamn world.

Hell, she'd even been furious with Spencer for believing that she'd willingly betray him. He should have known. He should have realized that someone was pulling her strings.

But he hadn't, and she'd moved like a zombie through her first year, only poking her head up at the end of the year when she finally found the strength to drop out. Spencer's show was on the air by then, though she'd only caught a few minutes of the first episode before realizing that it was far too painful to watch.

Still, she heard about the show. She knew that it was a runaway hit. That Spencer Dean had become a household name, with endorsements and a magazine and a book deal. She'd been so damn happy for him, and when Brian had called to say that he was in town, Brooke had immediately invited him to her apartment for drinks, eager for even that small bit of connection to the past—and to Spencer.

"Honestly, I haven't seen him in ages," Brian said when she asked about Spencer. "I've been working my ass off— I'm doing financial management now—and he's been so busy with the show." He shrugged. "You get it."

She'd agreed that she did, then offered him a drink while they caught up. They'd hung in her apartment, then gone to dinner, then returned for another drink. And maybe she should have shut it down sooner, but this was Brian. A constant presence in her life for as long as she'd known Spencer.

Maybe she shouldn't have invited him over.

Maybe she shouldn't have had that first drink.

Maybe if she'd done things differently, it never would have happened.

But it did.

She shuddered, blocking the hateful memory.

No. Dammit, it happened. It. Happened.

He'd slipped something into her drink. He'd ripped her choices away. He'd taken her control.

She would never—*ever*—forgive him for that.

But at the same time, she had to thank him, too. That one, horrible, awful night had changed her life. Shifted her perspective. And she'd ended up quitting medical school because fuck her parents and their puppet strings.

It had been her best decision ever. Now she had a business she loved. One that she ran. That operated based on her vision and her choices.

A business that Spencer was threatening.

Because this time it was Spencer who wanted to steal her control away.

Spencer, who wanted to punish her. Who wanted her at his mercy.

She trembled, the memory of his words once again taunting her. And the truth was, she wasn't sure she could meet his demands.

After Brian, she'd vowed never to never let a man take away her control again. But the truth was more ominous than that.

It wasn't about a vow. After all, vows could be broken.

No, it was *the idea* that terrified her. Made her insides clench. Her heart race.

Brian had made her scared to be vulnerable, and she hated him for it.

But at the same time, there was no going back.

So what the hell was she supposed to do now?

AMANDA HAD FOISTED a mimosa on Brooke, promising that it would ensure that she was relaxed for her lunch meeting. And, frankly, Brooke had to admit that her friend had a point. The drink had definitely taken the edge off of Brooke's trepidation, and she'd even managed to steer the conversation off of Spencer and the show and the impossible position she was in. But once she was back in her small Travis Heights bungalow to change clothes and gather her notes for the meeting, Brooke's nerves started to jangle again.

Any time I want.

Any way I want.

Complete control.

A hard shiver cut through her as Spencer's words filled her head, and she told herself she was worrying without reason.

Yes, he was being a ridiculous pig to put that kind of a condition on working with her, but that wasn't the issue.

The issue was whether she could do it, and the answer was yes. It had to be yes. Because she'd done it before. This was Spencer, after all. How many times had she given herself to him? Abandoned herself to his whims, his desire. Surrendered totally to his touch and his pleasure?

Too many times to count, and never once had he gone too far or pushed too hard.

But that was *before*.

Before she walked away.

Before Brian.

Before the thought of relinquishing control made her want to curl up into a small ball and hide.

She hadn't stayed cloistered these last five years, but she hadn't had a real relationship either. She didn't trust enough to open herself to that kind of intimacy. And as for pure sex—well, if a guy crossed the line, she ended it. *She* was the one in control. Always. Any shift in that dynamic, and she walked.

That was what control was all about, right?

Andrea, her therapist, had told her that there was nothing wrong with clinging tight to control early on if it eased the nightmares and the anxiety. And it had. After about a year, she'd felt mostly like herself again. The nightmares had faded, and she didn't end up in the bathroom having a panic attack every time she went to dinner or drinks with a guy.

But surrendering to a man in bed? Andrea might have urged her to begin opening herself up little by little, but that was an intimacy that she still wasn't prepared to give.

For a moment, she considered calling Andrea and getting her scoop on this whole mess. But the therapist had left Austin almost two years ago to take a position in Baltimore. She'd offered Brooke a referral, but Brooke had declined, assuring the older woman that she was feeling centered and whole again.

She'd meant it at the time. Now, though...

Now, she guessed that she'd have to rely on the Andrea that lived in her head.

The sharp ring of her doorbell saved her from getting lost in either her memories or her fears. "Coming!" she called as she hurried that way, wondering who the hell it could be at one o'clock on a Wednesday afternoon.

She pulled open the door, leaving the screen door latched, then froze. *Her father.*

"Daddy."

"Brooke." He didn't ask to come in, simply stood there as if it was his right. As if there was no question that she would let him in.

She unlatched the door and opened it for him.

She didn't see a lot of her parents, not in the last five years, anyway. But she also hadn't cut them off. As far as she knew, her mother had played no part in her dad's bid to end her wedding. And as for her father—well, he may have presented her with an impossible decision, but she'd been the one who made her choice. And while he hadn't been happy when she quit medical school, he had ultimately agreed that it was her life.

She'd accepted his grudging acquiescence, but they weren't close. And she knew they never would be again.

"The place looks good," he said as he strode past her into the living room. She cringed at the surprise in his voice but told herself to let it go.

"This is what I do, Daddy." So much for letting it go. "Did you think I was buying the place because it was cheap? Call me crazy, but I like floors and ceilings." The small house in the popular Austin neighborhood had been abandoned for years following an estate dispute. It had fallen into serious disrepair, but the bones were solid. And when Amanda had shown it to her, Brooke had fallen in love.

At the time, her remodeling company was still taking

off, so she'd had plenty of free time to put into the place. She'd remodeled the detached office first, then used it for meetings with potential clients, giving them a taste of what she and her crew were capable of. And every client who met her at the house had signed on the dotted line.

No doubt about it—she and the little house were good for each other.

Where she saw success and opportunity, though, her father saw lost dreams. "It's rather small," he said, looking around, and she knew that he was seeing the eight-bedroom Westlake mansion where he lived with her mother. A mansion bought with dollars earned from the law and a medical practice.

"It's plenty big for me, Daddy. Why are you here?" That came out rougher than she'd intended, but honestly, the man showed up unannounced on her doorstep and immediately began criticizing her house?

He fixed a sharp eye on her. The kind she'd seen him use from the bench to quell obnoxious attorneys or unco-operative witnesses.

"I don't mean to be rude," she hurried to say, even as she wanted to kick her own ass. "It's only that I have a meeting downtown in a few hours. I need to shower and change and—"

"Which is why I'm here."

Since he couldn't possibly mean the shower, she assumed he meant the meeting. She didn't question how he knew about it. Somehow, someway, her father knew about everything that went on within the Austin area.

She waited. There was no point in asking him what he meant. He'd come to her, and she knew damn well he wouldn't leave until saying his piece.

"I don't want you doing that show."

"Color me shocked."

"Don't be impertinent, young lady. You dodged a bullet when you left that hoodlum."

"*Left him?*"

"That is not a world you need to get drawn back into. He's knee deep in fraud allegations and tax evasion charges. I don't know the details yet, but I wouldn't be at all surprised if it ties into money laundering and a RICO conspiracy. Undoubtedly something the Crimson Eights are behind. Trust me, baby girl. Blood will tell. And that boy's blood is not something you want your name associated with. And you know damn well that if you do this show, the two of you will be splashed all over social media. Your past, Brooke. And your present. You do not want or need to be in with that boy like that."

Her throat tightened, not with concern about herself, but with fear for Spencer. She knew damn well he'd made some mistakes in his past, but he wasn't the kind of man who'd cheat on his taxes or launder money. And he sure as hell wouldn't get back in with a gang he'd spent the better part of his life avoiding.

Then again, you'd never have expected him to condition the show on sex. People change.

Maybe they did, but she didn't want to believe it.

Fuck.

"How do you know all of this? Those are federal claims, and you're a state court judge."

"Do you think I don't keep my ear to the ground? Especially where the man my daughter once ran around with is concerned?"

Ran around with.

Not *loved*. Not *almost married*.

It was as if her actions had never counted at all.

And maybe they hadn't. Maybe for years she'd been at the receiving end of bullshit.

Well, that ended today.

Spencer wanted to put some asinine condition on doing the show with her, then that was peachy-keen-okay by her. Because she had the power to walk away. But she was sticking because she wanted to. Not because he was forcing her, but because she'd weighed her options and balanced the scale.

This time *she* was making the choice. Spencer wasn't ripping control out of her hands the way Brian had. The way her father had over and over and over.

No, this time, Brooke was *giving* it to him. Handing him control so that she could get what she wanted. A calculated, reasoned, cold-blooded trade.

Which meant she wasn't surrendering it at all. *She* was the one manipulating the situation.

She was the white-hot goddess tugging on the strings that controlled the world.

And no one—not her father, not some dickless asshole with a stash of GHB, and not even Spencer—could take that from her. No matter how hard he fucking tried.

With a smile, she tilted her head up to meet her father's eyes. "Thanks for popping by, Daddy. But now I think you need to go."

Chapter Eight

AT A QUARTER TO ELEVEN, Spencer sat in the empty bar of The Driskill Hotel drinking a Scotch. He didn't usually drink before lunch, but he considered today a special occasion. The network meeting was in fifteen minutes, and Spencer still hadn't decided if he wanted Brooke to agree to his terms or to slap his face and run the other direction.

Honestly, it was a toss-up. And the Scotch wasn't helping.

For years, he'd been telling himself that he never wanted to see her again. Trying so damn hard to erase her from his thoughts.

And yet she'd lingered. He'd never managed to shut her out, and he'd spent the last five years comparing every other woman he dated to her.

With the exception that none of the women had left him at the altar, they'd all come up short by comparison.

Then again, he hadn't asked any of them to marry him either. Once bitten, twice shy, after all.

Not that any of the Hollywood women who'd latched

onto him would want him permanently. In their beds or on their arms, he was an interesting bauble to flaunt at the various network events and parties that had been command performances over the years. But he wasn't so naive as to think that any of those women would want something permanent with a guy like him. A guy who, at the end of the day, was a construction worker from a shit-hole neighborhood with a juvie record, gang connections, and a brother who'd narrowly escaped death row.

Yeah, he was one hell of a fucking awesome catch.

Once upon a time, he'd actually believed Brooke's bull-shit. That she wanted him. That she believed in him. That she saw all the work he'd put into making something of himself.

He'd thought she was his muse, and he'd known she'd be his wife. But on both counts, it had turned out to all be bullshit.

So, no. He wasn't a fucking awesome catch.

He was a fucking naive asshole.

Brooke had been playing a game with him. A bitter duel, but he'd been too blind to see when she pulled the trigger. And her bullet penetrated straight through his heart.

Yeah, she'd fucked him over, and good.

But now it was his turn.

He closed his eyes, remembering the heat of her when he'd cornered her at The Fix. He'd barely touched her and yet he'd *felt* her. The electricity of her. That vibrancy that he'd always associated with Brooke, like something restrained that longed to be set free.

Once upon a time, she'd let herself go in his bed. Had given in to that wildness that lived, untamed, inside her. And as much as she'd hurt him, he couldn't deny that it rankled to think that over the years she'd given herself like that to some other man. That another guy had felt the pulse of energy from the woman he'd once claimed as his.

Fuck.

That was exactly the kind of thinking he didn't need. Because, dammit, he didn't need her. Didn't want her. Not anymore. Not after she'd so callously walked away.

What he wanted was revenge. And the perfect plan had been laid in his lap.

He should be counting his blessings. After all, not many men had the chance to claim their life back, not to mention their balls.

It had been such a sweet moment. Her, trapped in his arms in that dark corner of the bar. Him, holding all fifty-two of the goddamn cards.

Terms he'd told her. He'd do the show, but only on his terms.

She'd managed to keep her expression blank; he'd give her credit for that. But he'd seen her swallow, and he'd reveled in that tiny show of fear. Then she'd asked that one, inevitable question: *What exactly do you want?*

He'd told her—*you*—and for just an instant he saw a light in her eyes. A light that looked remarkably like hope.

But then he'd showed his cards—*I want you at my mercy*—and he saw the light fade.

And for that one moment, he'd felt like the world's biggest heel.

That was okay, though, he thought as he stood and headed to the meeting.

He'd get over it.

"I HAVE to say that I'm very pleased you decided to accept our proposal and do the show." Molly, tall and Hollywood thin, flashed a smile that seemed a little too earnest. "I was always such a fan, and I hated the thought of you wasting all the goodwill you'd built up with your audience."

"Yeah," Spencer deadpanned. "I imagine that kept you up at night."

The truth was, Spencer did feel a twinge or two of guilt for walking away from the show. The fans—most of them at least—were legitimately interested in remodeling old houses. He'd received emails from all over the country asking his advice on varnish, paint colors, materials, and appliance selection. It was only when he was visiting LA that the whole thing seemed like a farce. There, the fans weren't fans at all. They were celebrity chasers. Women who wanted a piece of him, not a piece of advice.

Molly, who really wasn't an idiot, shot him the kind of look that suggested she'd read his thoughts exactly. To her credit, though, she didn't pursue the point. Instead, she passed him a folder with his contract, already vetted by Gregory. And now waiting for his signature and Brooke's as soon as she showed up.

Except Brooke was late.

Frowning, he glanced at his watch. Fifteen past eleven. Then he pulled his phone out of his pocket.

The same.

Interesting.

The suite included a small conference room, where Molly, Andy, and Spencer were seated. Now Molly stood up, then crossed to the window, looking down as if to track Brooke's progress.

"You may be out of luck," Spencer said. "I can't

imagine having me as part of the mix was appealing to her."

"I think having a show was appealing to her," Andy said, pushing John Lennon glasses up his nose.

Spencer shrugged, then glanced at his watch again. Another ten minutes, and he'd call it done, then consider himself lucky.

Except right then he didn't feel lucky. On the contrary, he felt hollow. Disappointed.

Frustrated, he pushed back from the table, then crossed to the window to stand beside Molly.

"She's probably stuck in traffic."

"You better hope so," Spencer said. "Because I'm sure as hell not doing this show alone. And it's looking more and more to me like I dodged a bullet."

He said the words with bravado even as he fought down a small knot of worry. Why the hell *wasn't* she here? Was it really traffic? Surely she hadn't been in an accident?

He did a mental eye roll. Christ, it was Austin. The city with traffic that rivaled Los Angeles, primarily because of all the damn Californians who kept moving to the city. Five minutes was nothing. She was probably stuck in construction on Mopac, one of the city's north-south freeways.

Which begged the question of why she'd be on that freeway at all, since she could get from her Travis Heights house to downtown on surface streets without getting anywhere near a freeway.

He had, of course, looked up where she lived. Just in case the information proved useful.

No, he wasn't worried that she was injured. He was afraid that he was about to lose a prime opportunity. She'd dropped a perfect scenario for revenge in his lap, and it would be one hell of a damn shame if he didn't get to enjoy yanking her chain.

That's all it was.

At least that's what he told himself. Because God knew he didn't want to do this show—hell, any show. And this wasn't about the chance to touch her again, no matter how much his body might tighten in response to the thought of having her in front of him, her eyes bright as she looked at him with longing, her lips parted with pleasure. And that low, sensual buzz that ran through him at the knowledge that she wanted him. *Him.*

He swallowed, his skin a little too warm and his jeans a little too tight.

Except she didn't want him. Never had. Not really.

And that's why this wasn't about romantic bullshit. This was about retribution. Revenge. It was about making her feel so damn good she wanted to scream, and then clearing the fuck out.

He needed to remember that. He needed to keep that at the forefront of his mind.

"Fuck," he said, turning away from the window. "Where the hell is she?"

"I'm here," Brooke said, stepping over the threshold and into the room, her business suit perfectly pressed and her chin held high. "Let's get to work."

Chapter Nine

BROOKE BARELY LOOKED at Spencer as Molly and Andy took them through the terms of the contract one more time, then had them both sign on the dotted line.

"This is going to be wonderful," Molly said. "Brooke, you'll let the folks at The Fix know that everything's in place?"

Brooke nodded. "I'm having lunch with Jenna Montgomery. I'll tell her. And I'll ask Tyree about having a small film crew there tonight for the first calendar contest."

"Just handhelds," Andy reminded her. "Totally unobtrusive. For that matter, tell him that when the remodel starts, we'll still be unobtrusive. This crew's worked several reality shows. They know how to blend."

Brooke nodded. The network wanted the Man of the Month calendar contest to be going on in the background of the show. That made sense, but considering the late start in getting the show off the ground, there was no way to include the contest for Mr. January during the renovations. So the crew was going to shoot footage now, and the editors would work it into the show. They didn't need much for the January contest, but at the very least they wanted shots of the contestants on the stage and the winning guy strutting his stuff.

And while they might not need Brooke for that, she fully intended to be there. Spencer, she assumed, would pass. He was a reluctant participant as it was. She figured she'd see him tomorrow at breakfast—their first official meeting.

And then, presumably, he'd want her to make good on his demand. Or condition. Or promise.

Or whatever the hell you wanted to call it.

Not that he'd said anything about that yet, but that wasn't surprising. He could hardly stop the meeting, point to Brooke, and tell her to be naked in his bedroom that night at midnight. Andy and Molly might not understand.

Dear God, she really needed to get out of her head.

The truth was, he might be planning on catching her after *this* meeting for that very thing. Which was why she pointedly glanced at her watch, then stood up with an announcement that she was late for lunch, and that since they all wanted to stay on the good side of everyone at The Fix, she really should run.

Then she bolted.

The coward's way out, perhaps, but she'd take it.

She met Jenna in the bar, then grinned like an idiot at Jenna's gleeful response to the news that everything was signed and ready to go. "And all I had to do was sell my soul."

"What?"

"Ignore me." Brooke waved the words away. "I was just trying to be funny."

They lingered a bit longer, then Jenna took Brooke to the owner, Tyree, a huge man with a kind smile who seemed genuinely grateful that *The Business Plan* was going to focus on his bar. "I've got my son, my friends, and this place. Losing any one of them would just about kill me. I'm doing whatever I can to make sure The Fix stays in business—and I think this show of yours is going to go a long way to making that happen."

"I hope so," Brooke said, touched. "That's certainly my plan."

She explained about the cameras that would be in place that night, and he told her that they could go anywhere and film anybody. "Jenna's a clever thing," he said. "For that matter, so is my lawyer, Easton. The contest is by ticketed entry only, and that ticket serves as consent to be filmed."

"Excellent." They talked over a few more details, including the mechanics of having the network confirm that Easton had covered all the legalities. Then she told him that she needed to go dive into prep, but that she'd be back that evening to watch the contest. "I wouldn't miss it even if I didn't need to see how the guys utilize the stage in order to better plan the renovation. I mean, a stage full of hot men? As far as I'm concerned, it's a no-brainer."

He chuckled, then walked her back into the main bar area. A few stragglers remained after lunch, but the place had mostly cleared out.

She'd been intending to go home and work, but right now, this felt as safe a place as any. And, more practically, she wanted to soak up more of the vibe.

The Fix had a comfortable local bar feel to it. Rough wood walls with neon signs advertising beers and a few

Texas license plates nailed to the walls. A vibrant mural spelling out AUSTIN filled the main wall of a front alcove near the beginning of the long oak bar that ran the length of the main room.

A stage near a corner of windows drew focus, but that performance space wasn't the heart of the establishment. On the contrary, The Fix was a bar with many hearts, which, Brooke decided, was one of the reasons it had such a varied clientele.

Folks came to The Fix for the amazing food, the incredible drinks, and the camaraderie. And whether the customers consisted of lawyers or students or construction workers, they all fit in, gathering in the various areas that management had set up. High- and low-tops filled the open area surrounding the stage. Comfortable bar stools lined the bar, giving the patrons a view of an amazing collection of liquors. A few small tables filled the alcove with the mural, and a long wooden bench ran in front of the window, so that patrons could pay attention to what was going on both inside and outside the club.

Further back, there was a second, smaller seating area. It boasted a full-service bar and tables as well. It even had a small stage that would accommodate a solo singer or musician. All in all, the place was about as perfect as a local bar could be, and the fact that it was in financial trouble only proved to Brooke that the locals were getting drawn to some of the corporate chain bars that had popped up like pimples lately for all the wrong reasons. Like dollar drinks that were watered down, flavorless, and utterly uninspired.

If her show could help bump up The Fix's cache in town, then she'd feel like not only had she accomplished something for her own business, but she'd done her good deed for the year.

"Hey, Brooke."

She glanced up to see Cameron, one of the bartenders she'd been introduced to recently, grinning at her.

"Huh?" She realized she'd been staring at the menu, completely zoning out. "Oh. Sorry. Thinking."

His smile widened, and she couldn't help but smile back. He was ridiculously good-looking in a boy-next-door kind of way, and he had some of the nicest eyes she'd ever seen. Someone, probably Jenna, had told her that he was in graduate school, though she had no idea what he was studying. But she assumed he studied hard. In only the short time that she'd been coming to The Fix, she'd seen at least a dozen girls hit on him, and as far as she could tell, he'd never taken the bait. She considered that he might be gay, but she'd also seen him hit on by guys, and as far as she could tell, nothing had happened there, either.

"I promise I'm not rushing you," Cam said. "We don't start charging rent for the stool until after you've sat for at least three days."

She laughed. "Good to know. And I'm ready. Just iced tea. And maybe some Boom Boom Shrimp to snack on. Too early to drink. I'll be under the table by tonight if I start now."

Then again, if Spence was going to make his demands on her tonight, maybe starting now would be a good idea. But no, sober was good. Sober was smart.

But what did he have planned?

For that matter, could she really handle this?

Determined, she clenched her hands at her sides, fighting a wave of nausea. This was Spencer, dammit. And she was making a choice. He wasn't taking; she was giving.

Giving, giving, giving.

No matter if the rat bastard believed otherwise.

Fuck.

Honestly, maybe she should get out of there. Go for a run. Do anything except think about tonight or tomorrow or whenever he intended to pounce.

Except then he'd have won, wouldn't he? Because he'd have kept her from doing her job. And it wasn't just her business that was depending on her. It was Tyree and Jenna and Cameron and everyone in this bar.

So fuck Spencer and his head games. Brooke Hamlin was getting to work.

She pulled out her notebook, intending to jot down a few thoughts, but ended up watching the folks in the bar instead, many of whom she'd seen before, and all of them looked at home. Something to keep in mind as she was remodeling. This was their place. She had to keep it familiar or risk ruining their experience.

At the end of the bar, a twenty-something man sat hunched over a notebook, his face hidden by the hood of an over-sized jacket. A woman with dark hair cut into a pixie style peered over his shoulder, talking and pointing at whatever was on those pages. After a moment, the guy nodded, and the girl hurried down the bar toward Brooke.

Her hair wasn't the only thing pixie-ish about her. She had high cheekbones, delicate features, and the prettiest green eyes that Brooke had ever seen. She climbed gracefully onto the stool next to Brooke, then turned her attention to Cam. "Hey, stranger," she said, and Brooke noticed that his ears went pink.

Brooke forced herself not to smile at that interesting development.

"Have you talked to Dickbreathe lately?"

Cam cocked his head, his usual self-possession return-ing. "You know, he's just going by Darryl these days. I figured you'd know that, what with being his sister and all."

"He hasn't paid me back for his half of Mom's birthday present. Until he does, he's Dickbreathe to me." She started to turn to Brooke, then obviously remembered something. "Oh! I forgot. Loser or not, I'm still throwing him a surprise birthday party when he comes home at the end of the semester. You'll come, right? My apartment. I mean, you have to be there."

"Oh, yeah, sure." His voice broke, and he cleared his throat, then smiled at her, a little shyly. "If I have to."

Her shoulder rose. "Well, yeah. You've been his best friend since forever. I mean, you're practically brothers. Which makes you my brother, too. Which means you really should chip in for the cake and alcohol." She waggled her brows. "I take checks and PayPal."

"Oh." He swallowed. "Right. Okay."

"Cam." She reached over the bar and closed her hand briefly over his. "I'm kidding."

As Brooke watched, red bloomed up Cam's neck to his ears and all the way to his forehead. The girl, thank good-ness, had already turned away, her effusive energy focused entirely on Brooke. Who, frankly, was already a little exhausted.

"I'm Mina," the girl said as Cam moved down to the far end of the bar. "Mina Silver. I'm a grad student at UT and Griffin's intern."

"And Cam's fake sister."

Her laughter bubbled out. "Cam's the best. He and my brother have been attached at the hip since they were kids, and I've been a pain in both their butts their whole lives. If I can't give my brother grief, Cam's the next best thing."

Since Mina seemed so completely earnest, Brooke decided not to tell her that Cam's feelings weren't quite as innocent. Even now, he'd probably disappeared into the break room to cast his hand in bronze. Or, possibly, to do other things with it.

Brooke shook her head—really not a mental picture she wanted at the moment.

"At any rate," Brooke said, "it's nice to meet you. I assume that's Griffin?" she added, nodding to the man in the hoodie.

"Yup," Mina said, then explained that Griffin was the writer, creator, and voice actor of a podcast that had skyrocketed in popularity. And the podcast had been turned into a similarly successful web series. "Thus, the needing of an intern. But he's between seasons now, and I'm looking for another gig. Rumor has it you're doing a reality show around The Fix."

"Um."

"And no pressure, but if you could use an intern, I'd love the gig. I'm pretty much willing to do anything. I need the experience—and I'd love to have something national to put on my resume."

Mina had completely charmed Brooke. "It's really not up to me. But I'll see what I can do."

"Really? That's terrific. Thanks so much." She handed Brooke a card with her cell number on it, said she was available anytime, then bounced back down to Griffin.

Considering Brooke had only been officially on the show for a few hours now, and she'd already lined up an intern, she was feeling pretty darned accomplished. She spent another couple of hours finishing her snack and adding to her notes, then she gathered up her things and headed home to change. For a moment, she considered not returning because Spencer might come to the contest tonight. More to the point, he might make demands tonight.

But she doubted it. He didn't want to do this program at all. The last thing he'd want to do was show up to work when he didn't have to.

Because officially on the clock or not, tonight was about working. Brooke intended to make sure the video crew got a good selection of footage—not just of the models, but also of the bar itself. She wanted to have plenty of clips to use in the episodes. Maybe even in the opening credits if Molly and Adam would entertain her suggestions.

Even if she was only sitting at the bar like she'd done this afternoon, that was work. As far as she was concerned, understanding the place she was going to remodel was as crucial as hammering that first nail.

So, yes, she was going back. And with any luck, Spencer was steering clear.

Luck, however, was a finicky bitch, and Brooke realized the moment she was back in the bar that evening that the bitch had it in for her. *Spencer was there.*

He hadn't seen her. Or, if he had, he hadn't acknowledged her. But he was there, larger than life. Just filling the room with that presence he had.

She longed to go to him. To cross back over the bridge of time to a moment when he didn't despise her.

But that was impossible. She could only go forward.

So she stuck to dark corners and avoided the man, grateful when the parade of very hot men across the poorly positioned stage finally began. She frowned and made a mental note: *Project One. Readjust the stage.*

She was considering angles—and wondering if some sort of rolling stage might be feasible—when Taylor, the woman Jenna had introduced as the stage manager she'd hired for the contest, came over to give Brooke a suggestion to pass onto the cameraman.

Their conversation froze, however, when the tattooed man that Brooke now knew was Reece got up on stage and gave the kind of heartfelt speech that made Brooke's toes curl, and her belly turn to goo. A speech filled with words like love and honor and relationship.

A speech he was making to Jenna.

Taylor pretty much sprinted for the spotlight, then turned and shined it straight on Jenna, whose face glowed with so much love it made Brooke's heart hurt.

"That was the most romantic thing ever," she said when Taylor came back.

"I know, right?"

"Listen, I'll see you tomorrow, okay? I need to go."

Taylor's forehead creased. "You okay?"

"Just a headache." That, of course, was a lie. Reece's words of love and devotion had only underscored what Brooke had once shared with Spencer—and what she'd lost.

And no matter what Spencer might be planning, Brooke didn't think she could handle it tonight. Not with those words in her head.

"I'll be fine," she assured Taylor, who was offering to get her some Ibuprofen from the First Aid kit. "I'll see you tomorrow," she added, then took a step toward the door.

But she didn't get that far. A perky blonde that Brooke

didn't recognize told her that the man with the beard and the leather jacket wanted to see her.

Spencer.

"Tell him I'm not feeling well," she replied. "Tell him I'm going home."

"Sure," the girl said, then slipped back into the crowd as Brooke hurried the other direction, pushing through the crowd and hating herself for being a coward. But she couldn't deal. She just couldn't.

With relief, she reached the solid oak doors. She drew a breath, looked back over her shoulder to make sure Spencer wasn't there, then pushed the door open and stepped out onto Sixth Street.

And there was Spencer.

She had no idea how he'd managed to slip outside—he must have gone into the back bar and used the side entrance. But the moment she saw him with that determined expression, she felt her whole body go weak.

He stood silently as she stayed frozen in place. His brown eyes skimmed over her, his expression hard and possessive, his mouth curved into a derisive smile.

"Spencer, I—"

"No," he said, two fingers going over her lips to hush her. And then, before she could even make sense of what was happening, his mouth closed over hers, his tongue demanding entrance as his beard teased her lips and her skin.

She gasped, her body reacting immediately to this man whose touch she knew so well. He heard it and took advantage, his hand cupping her ass to pull her close so that she could feel the press of his erection against her lower belly. His other hand tight at the nape of her neck, holding her still as his tongue tasted and took, making her melt even as she wanted to cry out that it wasn't fair. She'd had no time to put up any defenses at all.

Then it was over.

He pushed away, his expression cocky, as onlookers on the street clapped and whistled. She stood perfectly still, breathing hard, not sure if she should run or slap his face.

"Come on, baby," he said, reaching for her hand. "It's time."

Chapter Ten

SPENCER LED her across the street to The Driskill Hotel, then up to a suite just two floors above where they'd met that afternoon.

He opened the door to reveal a dark sitting room illuminated by the glow of a single desk lamp. A champagne bucket stood next to the sofa, a bottle chilling inside. And two champagne flutes sat on the coffee table on either side of a serving tray of artfully placed cheeses.

He held the door open, ushering her inside. "Pretty, isn't it? I thought it was appropriate."

Brooke's breath caught in her throat and she forced herself to keep her voice steady. "Appropriate?"

"Don't you remember? We came to The Driskill on our third date. We had a drink at the bar, and then we got a room. We couldn't keep our hands off each other, and I had you naked mere seconds after the door closed behind us."

"Of course I remember," she snapped, her eyes cutting to him. "Do you really hate me that much?"

She thought she saw something flicker across his face.

Regret or some other indefinable emotion. Then his expression hardened, and she wondered if it had been only shadows from the candlelight.

"Hate?" He crossed to the sofa and sat, then patted the seat next to him so that she could sit beside him.

She hesitated, then complied. That was the point, right? The reason she'd come. To give in to him. To do what he said so that he would do the show.

"Hate?" he repeated, this time sounding thoughtful. "What is hate but the other side of love?" He put his hand on her leg, just above the hem of her skirt, and she felt her body respond. Threads of electricity that shot through her, making her ache with long-remembered desire. Making her crave the touch of the Spencer she'd once loved with all of her heart and soul.

She was wearing a simple cotton skirt and a button-down blouse that she'd picked to wear to The Fix. She wanted to look both like she belonged at a bar and professional. If she'd realized Spence was going to lay his claim tonight, she'd have considered pants and a long-sleeve shirt. Boots, too.

Gently, he eased up the skirt's hem, his thumb dancing along her skin in a sensual pattern that was making her body respond even while her mind tried to clamp down. Tendrils of desire twirled through her, and she felt a keen ache of longing building in her breasts and between her thighs.

Damn him—and damn her body for remembering the touch of a very different Spencer.

She fought a whimper as his hand eased higher up her thigh, his fingertip teasing close to the edge of her panties.

"And trust me, baby. I don't love you anymore." Slowly, he drew his hand higher, his finger moving along the elastic band as she sat stiff as a board, trying not to react. "So how could I possibly hate you?"

The words seemed to reach out to her, squeezing her heart painfully.

She closed her eyes, wishing she weren't in this room with him. Wishing everything was different.

"Look at me."

There was a softness in his voice that unnerved her, and she turned her head to comply. His mouth made a dangerous slash beneath his beard. His brown eyes burned as hard as stone. Whatever tenderness she'd imagined wasn't apparent in his face. On the contrary, he was looking at her with such a fierce intensity she had to fight the urge to get up and leave.

That's what he wanted, of course. He wanted out. Out of the show. Away from her.

A heartbeat passed with their eyes locked on each other. Then he slowly looked down, not in defeat, but as if that part of the game was up and he was moving on to the next challenge. She exhaled, not realizing she'd been holding her breath. She felt all twisted up. This man beside her was *Spencer*, dammit. A man who once would have laid down his life for her.

Now, he wanted to destroy her.

She'd done that.

For a moment, she considered telling him the truth. She could explain what had happened. The bargain she'd made with the devil on Richie's behalf. Maybe now, her father wouldn't leak his record. Or, maybe now Spencer wouldn't care if he did.

But she couldn't make herself say the words. She'd made that sacrifice for a different man—not the Spencer who sat beside her playing emotional and sexual games.

"I think it's time to see what I've been missing all these years. Stand up, baby, and strip for me."

He said the words as casually as if he were ordering a sandwich. Then he reached over and poured a glass of champagne. He held it out to her, but she kept her hands firmly at her sides. He shrugged, then swallowed. "Liquid courage," he said. "I thought it might help."

"Fuck you," she said, then stood and walked in front of him. He'd seen her naked hundreds of times. So why not strip for him now? It didn't mean anything, after all. Nothing except that he was a manipulative prick, and she was a woman who'd sacrificed her pride for the sake of her business.

But she could live with that. She'd gone in with eyes open, after all.

"Is this the kind of man you are now?" she asked as her fingers went to the buttons on her blouse.

"Don't pretend like you don't know what kind of man I am. What kind of man I've always been."

"What the hell is that supposed to mean?"

"A guy who's all wrong for a girl like you. Wrong family. Wrong neighborhood. Wrong dreams."

Temper flared. "That's bullshit, and you—"

"Strip," he said, cutting her words off with one tight, harsh syllable.

She wanted to argue, but he simply pointed to her now unbuttoned shirt.

She shrugged out of it, letting the silk fall to the floor. "I damn sure never expected you to be the kind of man who pouts."

His brows rose. "Pouts?"

"Yeah. You didn't get your way and so now you have to humiliate me."

"Didn't get my way?"

She heard the hard edge in his voice and knew she'd crossed into dangerous territory.

"Take off the fucking skirt, baby."

She considered protesting, but one look at the hard lines of his body changed her mind. She tugged down the zipper, then let the skirt fall to the ground over her hips, leaving her clad in bra, panties, and a pair of high heeled pumps.

"Christ. You're still as beautiful as you were back then."

She heard the catch in his throat and saw the softening of his features. And right then, she thought that maybe—maybe—her Spencer was in the room with her after all.

"Spence? Please."

His eyes cut up to hers, and they were as hard as steel. "We'll save the rest. I think I might finish getting you naked with my teeth."

For a moment—one brief, wonderful, horrible moment—she imagined the feel of him on top of her. His mouth tugging down her bra, his beard rough against her tender skin. Then his body moving lower as he spread her legs and tugged her panties down with his teeth, just far enough so that he could expose her before his tongue did all those miraculous things she remembered.

She shivered—and she hated herself for it. All the more when he noticed.

"I'm cold," she said.

"Don't worry, baby. I'm about to warm you up."

She swallowed. "So that's your plan? You're just going to use me?"

His brows rose. "Isn't that what you're doing with me?"

She didn't answer, because what the hell could she say to that?

He stood, then came to her, standing mere inches in front of her. He reached out to touch her breast, taking her nipple between two fingers. She closed her eyes, forcing herself to keep her body stiff. To not react.

It didn't work. She felt desire well inside her, and hated herself for it. She didn't want him—or, did she? She wanted *Spencer*. Not this man determined to torment her. But her body made no distinction, and as his hand traced slowly down her bare skin, a matching desire rose within her.

Gently, he stroked her breasts, then teased a finger down to her navel, then lower still until his hand slipped between her thighs to cup her sex. "You're wet," he murmured, and she wished she could tell him he was wrong, but it wasn't true. She hadn't reacted to a man like this in years. And, she knew, she wasn't even reacting to this man. This was about the man who lived in her memories. A man she missed desperately.

"Open your eyes."

She did, and for a moment he was her Spencer again, and she wanted to cry with relief.

"Spencer, I—"

"Bedroom," he said, and once again the heat of memory was buried beneath the chill of his voice.

"Bedroom," she repeated, then moved that direction. She told herself this would be okay. *She* would be okay. This was a commercial transaction—sex for the show.

Then she saw the bed, and a wild shiver cut through her body. *She shouldn't have agreed to this. Oh, dear God, she should never have said this was okay.*

It was a four-poster bed, and black silk ties extended from each of the four posts. A leather paddle and a fur mask sat innocently on the pillows.

She blinked, trying to process what she was seeing. He wanted to tie her up?

Of course, he did. He'd said he wanted her at his mercy, didn't he?

Oh, God. Oh, Christ.

A wave of panic washed over her. She'd tricked herself into coming here by deluding herself that she was in control. But that was bullshit. She wasn't in control. She wasn't even close to being in control.

She couldn't do this. She *really* couldn't do this.

She'd walked away from Spencer five years ago, and she should have stayed away. Far, far away.

"On the bed, baby."

She opened her eyes to see Spencer leaning against the doorframe, studying her. She tried to keep her expression neutral, but it was hard, so damn hard to fight the panic that was rushing up, threatening to spill out in tears and wails to please, please, please let her go home.

No. She could do this.

She had to do it.

"On the bed," he repeated, and she nodded, then took a tentative step that direction. She would *not* cry. She would do it. She owed him this. After all, this was the bargain they made.

She pressed a hand to the mattress, intending to climb onto the bed, but then his voice stopped her.

"Wait. Stand up."

She did as he said, standing stiff as he came closer. She flinched a little, expecting his touch, but he stood arms length away, those dark eyes once again raking over her, undoubtedly imagining all the things he was going to do to her when she was tied to that bed and helpless.

"Get dressed," he said, and for a moment she saw the Spencer she used to know reflected in those eyes.

"I—what?"

His expression cleared, unreadable once more. "The meeting's at nine tomorrow at The Fix, right? I'll see you there." Then he walked out of the room without waiting for her to answer.

Brooke didn't remember her knees giving out, but the next thing she knew she alone in the room, her butt planted firmly on the plush, carpeted floor as her heart pounded with relief—and her head wondered what the hell it could mean.

Chapter Eleven

HE WAS A SHIT. A heel. A goddamn horrible person.

He'd been so fucking angry with her. Had he actually believed that torturing her would make it better? All it had done was make it worse because he'd seen her pain and it had just about ended him.

Do you really hate me that much?

Her words echoed in his mind, each syllable like a fucking knife to his heart. Because no, he didn't hate her. And maybe that was the trouble. He wanted to hate her— Christ, he'd wanted to hate her since the day she walked away—but she was too far under his skin, too deep in his system.

He loved her—at least he had once. Maybe he still did. He didn't know anymore. All he knew was that he damn well didn't deserve her. Never had.

Fuck.

He scrubbed his palms over his face and leaned back against the Drysdale Mansion's moldering wood paneling.

He shouldn't have come here tonight. Honestly, he

wasn't sure why he had. He should have known it would only make the craving worse. A longing for the home he'd never have, the past he couldn't fix, and the woman who'd never be his.

With a sigh, he tilted his head back, wishing for another time, another place. Another set of goddamn circumstances.

But he knew better than to believe in hopes and wishes. They so rarely came true.

Sometimes they did, though.

He thought of Richie, so close to the surface of Spencer's thoughts, as he always was when Spencer was in this house. Or feeling lost and angry.

In so many ways, Richie had been the voice of reason in Spencer's ear. "Don't ever do something just to go along, little brother. You know your own mind, and that's the path you need to be walking. I veered. And I got my ass kicked good and solid. Don't be me, okay?"

It was Richie who'd told Spencer to get his shit together after he dropped out of high school. Richie who'd urged him to keep up the battle to get *Spencer's Place* made. Who'd told him that Brooke was a hell of a catch, a woman worth fighting for.

Hell, he'd even said the same after she walked away, only Spencer was too blind with grief to listen and had called his brother a goddamn fool.

Not that it would have mattered. She'd left him, after all. And he wasn't about to go crawling back to her, begging her to love him. Not when she'd so definitively made her choice.

A sharp *clank* from the kitchen had him on his feet. Probably a raccoon—the gate, he knew, was locked up tight. He'd seen to that after he'd picked the thing to get in. He was alone; he was sure of it.

Even so, he reached into his boot and pulled out the knife he kept tucked in there.

He stood still, barely breathing, and then cursed silently when he heard footsteps. *Dammit.* Might be kids who'd scaled the gate, but he didn't need this shit tonight.

He took a step toward the kitchen, intending to scare them off before they did even more damage to the ailing old house.

Then he saw her. *Brooke.* Standing in the archway between the living area and the dining room. She wore jeans now, paired with a black pullover, and her long, blonde hair spilled over her shoulders.

The light from a full moon streamed in through the missing chunks of roof, making her hair shine like a halo, a sharp contrast to the dark-clad body. She looked ethereal. Beautiful.

And for the length of a heartbeat, he thought that his wish had come true, and they'd traveled back five years to the time when she was still his.

Then she spoke, and the spell was broken. "Who's there?"

He heard the fear in her tone and realized that she hadn't come there looking for him. *Interesting.* He slipped the knife back into his boot, then stepped forward, out of the shadows.

"Brooke," he said. "It's me."

"Spencer?" She glanced side to side, looking spooked. "I didn't expect you to be here. I—"

"I know." He took a step closer.

"No, please. Don't." She met his eyes. "It's okay. I'll go."

Something tight twisted around his heart. He couldn't let her go. Not like this. Not when it felt like fate had brought her here to give him a way to hoist himself out from the giant hole he'd dug for himself. "Please," he said. "Stay."

She wrapped her arms around her chest. "I needed—I mean, I wanted to be alone."

Fuck. That was on him. Because he'd been a prick.

"Considering I'm not much of a human right now, much less a man, you pretty much are alone with me."

A whisper of a smile played at her lips. "I kind of hate you right now."

The words were a relief. "You should," he said. "I hate myself, too. I'm a fucking lowlife prick. And about a million other horrible things."

"No argument here."

She glanced behind her, but didn't turn to leave. *Good*. Right then, the thing he wanted most in the world was for her to stay. For her to see him as Spencer again, and not as the fucking idiot he'd been the last few days.

"How'd you get in? Did you remember what I taught you?"

This time, the smile was genuine, and he felt like a goddamn hero for bringing it to her lips. "I do remember, but I was only ever any good when you were with me."

He knew she was talking about picking a lock, but the words burned through him, full of meaning. He cleared his throat, knowing he was reading too much. Hoping too much. "So if you didn't pick the lock, how'd you get in?"

"The real estate agent who listed this place—Amanda —she's one of my closest friends. I took a guess at the lockbox code, and I got it right."

"Also a useful tool for anyone trying to break into a rundown old mansion. Know your mark."

"Yeah, well, I'm not sure Amanda really qualifies as a mark. But as for the rundown part..." She glanced around. "It's gotten a bit worse for wear since we were here last, hasn't it?"

His heart tightened as memories of the two of them together in this house swelled inside him. So much they'd had together. And so much they'd lost.

Tonight, he'd tried to punish her for that, but maybe it was on him, too. He hadn't fought, he'd simply accepted. He'd been so goddamn furious when she'd said she was leaving him that he just let her go.

"I'm sorry," he said, putting everything he felt behind the words.

She tilted her head. "You should be. What exactly are you apologizing for?"

"Right now? I'm apologizing for tonight. For being an asshole. For turning what I felt for you into a game and trying to punish you for leaving me. It killed me, you walking away. But it was your choice, and what I did was unforgivable."

"Choice," she whispered, so softly that he wasn't even certain that she realized she'd spoken the word.

"You chose a life without me, and then when the network told me I had to do the show with you, it was another goddamn choice that I didn't get to make. So I decided to act like a petulant baby who didn't get his own way. It's not an excuse, I know. But maybe it's an explanation." He sighed. "Does that make any sense at all?"

For a long time, she said nothing. Then she met his eyes. "Yeah. I get that. It's not easy giving up control, especially when you don't have any choice in the matter."

She looked away quickly, staying just out of arm's length as she walked past him, then crawled up into the window seat where they used to sit to look out at the garden. "So, you're saying I was right?"

He jerked his head up sharply. "About what?"

"What I told you in the hotel room—that's not the kind of man you are."

"Who fucks women to get what he wants? Who humiliates them and forces them into untenable situations because he's not man enough to suck it up and deal with the fact that his heart got broken?" He shrugged. "I wouldn't have thought that was me. But then you walked back into my life. And I went a little bit off the rails."

Her brows rose. "A little bit?"

"A lot. But you always did inspire large gestures from me."

She laughed. A full-on, genuine laugh. And some of the ice around his heart melted.

"Brooke." He heard the need in his voice, then closed his mouth with a shake of his head. He wasn't going to ask why. He wasn't going to destroy this moment. Instead he said, "I've missed you."

"I know. I've missed you, too."

Her voice was so soft that he was afraid he hadn't heard right.

"What?"

"Well, not the you from the last couple of days." She lifted her brows as if to punctuate the point. "But the real Spencer. I miss him."

He almost snapped that she'd have the old Spencer if she hadn't walked out on their wedding, but he kept his anger in check. This, after all, was progress. So all he said was, "Oh."

He moved to stand beside her, then nodded at the seat. She hesitated, then pulled up her feet to make a space for him.

The silence hung between them once again as thick as the dust in the air. Finally, Spencer cleared his throat. "I went and saw Richie. After you left."

"After he got clemency," she said. "Of course, you would have." A blush rose on her cheeks. "I did, too."

The revelation startled him. "You—what? Why?"

She lifted one shoulder. "It was a few weeks later. I-I always liked Richie."

"He liked you, too. Told me I should fight for you."

"Did he?" She rested her chin on her knees. "Why didn't you?"

"Would it have done any good?"

He saw the flicker of something that looked like pain on her face. "No," she whispered.

"I didn't think so. And honestly, back then I wasn't sure I wanted to."

"No." She licked her lips. "Of course, you wouldn't have."

"Right." He wiped his hands on his jeans, feeling ten kinds of awkward. She was right there, just inches from him. The woman he craved with all his heart and soul— and he was making fucking small talk. "So, you saw Richie," he prompted because right then, that was the best he could think of.

"Yeah. I would have gone sooner but, I was afraid I might see you there, and—"

"Yeah. Couldn't have that."

"No," she whispered. "I was afraid I couldn't bear it."

He wanted to cry out that she'd been able to stand being with him for the two years they'd dated. Sleeping in his bed. Squeezing every bit of satisfaction from him as she screamed his name over and over in pleasure. *That* she could handle, but seeing him would have killed her. Because she'd had her epiphany. She'd realized what a fool she'd been, and she'd run away from him far and fast.

But all he said was, "Why did you go see him?"

Another little shrug. "I had my reasons. Mostly, I wanted to see that he was okay." She licked her lips. "And I thought he would know if you were okay. I couldn't imagine that you wouldn't have been by to see him yet."

"I had. I told him everything. Pretty goddamn selfish of me considering all he'd just been through, but then again, there's only so much you can say after *thank God you're still alive*. Well, thank God and the governor, anyway."

"Right," she said, her face tilted down as she twisted her fingers together. He frowned as a chill raced up his spine. Something was off. He just couldn't figure out what. "Brooke?"

When she lifted her face, he saw tears in her eyes.

"Brooke?" he repeated. "What is it?"

"It's just so tragic, what happened to him. And I was so relieved when his sentence got commuted." She flashed a smile, a smile that looked forced. "I'm just emotional, is all."

He didn't believe her, but he wasn't going to press. God knew, he'd pressed her enough that night.

He shifted on the seat, maneuvering into a more comfortable position. The seat was designed for two, but it was still crowded, especially if the two were adults trying very hard not to touch each other. When he was resettled, he realized that his leg was bumping up against hers.

And, having noticed it, that one tiny point of connection was all that he could think about.

"How's your dad?" she asked, apparently unaffected by their contact.

"He's doing okay. Mentally, he's still gone most days, but there are some good ones when he remembers me. Some bad ones when he only thinks about Richie." He'd had a stroke after Richie's first appeal had been denied, and had been in a nursing home ever since. "He's been in that home for years now," Spencer said with a shake of his head. "It's the longest he stayed in one place his whole life."

His father had never had a place of his own. He'd dragged Richie and Spencer from rental to rental, sometimes living out of a toolshed while he did renovation work on someone's house. Always building or fixing a home for someone else, never for himself or his family. Not enough money. Not enough time.

The irony was that now Spencer was nomadic, bunking with friends from the old neighborhood while he waited for title to the mansion, not wanting to spend a dime of his remaining cash on something as ridiculous as rent.

"I'm sorry," she said, but he just shrugged.

"We live a hard life, we Dean men. My dad worked his ass off, even if he never got the golden ticket."

"He did a good job with you."

Spencer ran his fingers through his hair. He'd forgotten how easy she was to talk to. How much he enjoyed just having her beside him. "He tried, that's for sure. And how did I repay him? I dropped out of the school he and Richie worked so hard to get me in."

"Cut yourself some slack. We both know there were extenuating circumstances. Your brother had just been sent up. Then later, your dad got ill. But you got your shit together, Spence." She shifted, the denim of her jeans scraping against his. "You made something of yourself."

"Did I?" He met her eyes, hyperaware of her proximity. Of the contact between them. "All I can do is work with my hands. All that corporate bullshit? The financial planning? It's a fucking nightmare to me, and that makes me weak."

"Nobody likes that stuff."

"Do you know why I'm doing this show?"

"Because you owe them one show under your contract."

"True, but that's not the reason. I've been paying for his care. So he's got a decent room, you know? And then *boom*, the money's gone. Because I fucked up and didn't pay enough attention to my own damn finances. I need this show to keep him in decent digs. Otherwise, he gets shipped off to another facility across town, and I'm pretty sure they won't put fresh flowers in his room every day."

"I had no idea." She leaned forward and took his hands, and the shock of connection went through him like a bolt of lightning. "You're a good son. A good man."

"Yeah, I sure as hell proved that today, didn't I?"

"You were an ass, today," she said baldly. "But it's almost midnight. So you can start fresh."

He met her eyes, blue ice flashing in the moment. "Can I?" he asked, his voice cracking with the words.

He felt need tighten in his chest. His head was spinning, and some annoying voice in his head was saying that it was too fast. But five years didn't seem fast. Five years seemed like a hell he was ready to climb out of.

"Can *we* start fresh?" he asked, the question almost a whisper.

"I—Spencer." She swallowed, but she didn't say yes. Then again, she didn't say no, either.

"I'm going to kiss you, now," he murmured, desperate to taste her. "Not because I want to punish you. But because I want you. And if that's a problem," he added, as he leaned toward her, "you better stop me now."

Chapter Twelve

I'M GOING to kiss you now.

The words rumbled through Brooke, filling and teasing her, warm and wild and delicious.

She leaned forward, knowing that she shouldn't want this. There'd been so much pain between them. So many lost opportunities. And way too many secrets.

She'd missed him so much—so damn much. The Spencer who'd been her lover and her friend. For years, she'd lived with the knowledge that she'd lost him forever. And then when he'd made his horrible demand, she'd been certain of it.

But here they were, and she realized for the first time that he'd been as lost tonight as she'd been. Both of them clawing their way through years of loss and longing.

Maybe he was still unreachable. Maybe they'd never truly be able to make it right.

But for the first time, she had the chance to capture a bit of the past. And that wasn't a chance she was going to walk away from. Not when she craved him so much. When she could barely catch her breath, and when her pulse skittered beneath her skin, alive with desire.

Gently, he cupped her chin, those brown eyes searching her face. She knew what he saw. Fear, longing, and just a little bit of daring.

Slowly, she curved her mouth into a smile. "I'm not saying no," she whispered.

"Thank God," he said, then kissed her. Not the wild, demanding kiss she'd been expecting. No, this was gentle. Almost sweet. His lips brushing over hers. His tongue tasting.

His hand closed at the nape of her neck, pulling her closer, his thumb stroking as his mouth moved tenderly over hers, his beard tickling her mouth and her cheeks.

He was taking his time, and she let herself settle in, tasting him and remembering all the times he'd touched her. Kissed her. His hands exploring. His mouth demanding.

The heat of those memories rushed through her, and she wanted more. She craved the realization of those memories now, in the present. She wanted him to claim her mouth. To take what she was giving. To kiss her so thoroughly it erased all the bad memories and all the loss.

"Spencer," she murmured against his mouth, and that was all it took. He knew what she wanted, just as he'd always known.

His fingers knotted in her hair, and he tugged her head back, his lips moving from her mouth to her throat as she shivered with pleasure, her entire body warming up, like an ember about to burst into flame.

His lips traveled up her sensitive skin to her ear, where he teased the curve with his tongue, then whispered her name, his voice infused with so much heat that she felt her sex tighten and pulse with desire.

He traced kisses over her temple, brushed gentle lips over her eyes, and then attacked her mouth once again, in a take-no-prisoners kind of kiss. Tongue and teeth and desire and possession, it was all there in a kiss as intimate as sex. A kiss that claimed and took and *owned*.

And, still, she wanted more. "Yes," she said. "God, yes."

He pulled away, gasping.

"Spencer." His name was a plea; her tone a whimper. "Please."

He shook his head. "I left you in The Driskill after I caught the look on your face when you saw the bed."

She swallowed, then glanced down, afraid that he would ask what had put that fear on her face.

"Brooke?" His thumb traced her jawline. "Angel, please look at me."

Slowly, once she knew she'd pulled herself together, she lifted her eyes to him. "I don't have that look now."

"No, you don't, and I'm so glad. But I want you to be certain. Ready. Are you?"

She considered the question. She wanted to be—good God, her body wanted it so damn badly. But sleeping with him now would be sleeping with a memory. If—and it was a big *if*—they were going to move forward, it wouldn't be with a ghost.

She drew in a breath, then shook her head a tiny bit. "I should get home," she said. "If I don't go now, I'll end up wearing these clothes to tomorrow's meeting. And I don't think that would scream professionalism."

"You look great." His quick grin flashed with amusement. "But I see your point."

She slid off the window seat, then smoothed her clothes. Then she reached for Spencer's hand and squeezed it, just a little. "Thank you," she said, and then hurried for the door before she changed her mind.

———

BRENT SINCLAIR OPENED the door to his cute little bungalow sporting a dishtowel over one shoulder and a teddy bear clutched in the crook of his arm.

"Will he be leading our meeting?" Brooke asked, smiling. She didn't know Brent well yet, but Jenna had introduced her to all of the players at The Fix, so Brooke knew that he was one of the owners and was in charge of the bar's security. And if she hadn't already known he was a single dad, the sight of a teddy and Brent's harried expression would have suggested as much.

"Come on in," he said, pulling the door the rest of the way open to usher her in. "Sorry for the craziness, and thanks for agreeing to meet here. I know it's not ideal."

"It's no problem."

"My daughter spiked a fever last night. She's doing okay today, but there's a twenty-four hour no-fever policy at her kindergarten, and my babysitter's not available."

"Really, it's fine. To be honest, I love driving in this neighborhood. Crestview has some great restored houses." She glanced around at the small, but well-designed house. "Someone did a great job with the built-in cabinets and bookshelves."

"Someone not me," Brent said. "I bought it fixed up. Diapers, play dates, surveillance, and bad guys I've got the hang of."

"Bad guys?"

"Ex-cop," he said. "Law and order I can do. But I'm mostly clueless at Home Depot. That's more Reece's territory."

He cocked his head toward the back. "We're in the dining room. Head on back through the kitchen and help yourself to some coffee. I've got to give Faith her little friend and then I'll be right there."

Brooke gave him a thumbs-up and hurried that direction, wondering if she'd beat Spencer. But the second she stepped into the kitchen, she knew that he'd arrived first. Not that she saw him. No, she just *felt* him. His presence. His energy.

And when she moved through the kitchen area, then turned into the small attached dining room, there he was, standing in the corner laughing with Reece and Jenna.

He held a cup of coffee and took a sip from it. As he did, his gaze cut to Brooke over the rim of the mug, and though she couldn't see his mouth, she saw the smile in his eyes, and crossed to him, drawn inexorably to him as if he were a magnet and she was solid steel.

"Hey," she said.

"Hey, yourself." Pretty basic as conversations went, and yet there was a familiar heat in those words that shot all the way to her toes. His free hand moved to rest on her lower back, and she took a step closer to him. It felt comfortable, like coming home.

Slow, she reminded herself. *You're supposed to be taking it slow.*

Wise words, but she didn't heed them. Didn't step away into her own space. Instead she stayed, secure in that gentle touch, and joined in the conversation, which was meandering between kids and cars and the best places in town to grab breakfast.

"Sorry about that," Brent said, coming into the dining room with Molly and Tyree right behind him. "We're all here now, and Faith's settled in with *Blue's Clues*, so I think we're good to go."

Tyree spoke as they all grabbed a seat at the dining room table, to which some folding chairs had been added to make room for everybody. "I want to say how grateful I am—we are," he amended, indicating Reece and Brent and Jenna, "that you're doing the show. It's not something I would have thought of, but I've got to say I can see how it could bring in the customers. And that's my bottom line these days."

"And *our* bottom line is viewers," Molly said. "So it works out well for us, too. Your bar has a great look, and yet it can benefit from a remodel. And you have the Man of the Month contest going on. I won't deny that was a big part of our decision-making process."

Across the table, Jenna buffed her nails on her chest, making Reece laugh. Brooke had never asked, but she assumed the calendar contest was Jenna's idea.

"Shouldn't Andy be here?" Brooke asked, suddenly realizing that only Molly was representing the network. "For that matter, shouldn't the crew be here as well?"

Molly shook her head. "Andy's back in LA, so I'll be your in-town contact. And as for the crew, we like to do reality shows with as limited a crew as possible, and no interaction from the on-camera talent. That means that I'm not even going to introduce you to our camera guys—and they'll be using very unobtrusive handhelds for the most part." She turned to Tyree. "I would like to set up a few permanent cameras, if that's okay. Mount them near the ceiling, maybe a few eye-level locations. We can pull footage as needed."

The big man held up his hands. "Whatever you need."

"One of the regulars asked me about being an intern," Brooke said.

"That must be Mina," Reece guessed. "She works for Griffin, but has less to do when he's between seasons."

"I'm guessing the answer is no since there's a limited crew?"

Molly lifted a shoulder. "We can give her a camera. The more footage the better. And there are minor jobs that will need to be done. Give her my number and I'll talk to her."

"Thanks," Brooke said, already feeling proprietary about the eager grad student.

"That's all for me," Molly said, holding up her hands. "Brooke, do you want to run through what the plan is for the renovation and how it breaks down into our episodes?"

"Sure." She shot a quick glance to Spencer. "I put together a lot of this before you were on board. If you have changes or—"

"I'm sure it's fine. Dive in. I'll comment if I have something to say."

"And this is where I feel guilty again," Brent said. "I'm sure this would be much easier if we were in the actual bar."

Brooke waved a hand, dismissing his words. "Nobody knows the place better than you do, and if you guys can't figure out what I'm talking about from my sketches, then I need to work on my presentation skills."

She opened her portfolio and began to pull out her mock-ups, starting with the stage. "Since you use the stage for the contest and for performances, I'd like to completely demo what's in place now and put in a larger stage, only in removable sections, like this." She pulled out a few other sheets, showing how the pieces of the envisioned stage would fit together like a jigsaw puzzle.

"We can do the same thing with seating, too. Have some tables that fold and combine to be either two or four tops, some even combining to seat eight. Basically the idea is to maximize as much space as possible. The more customers the better, right?"

She looked up to meet all their eyes and saw that everyone was looking back at her with interest. Except for Spencer—his eyes were full of pride, and she felt a surge of pleasure at having impressed him.

So much that it knocked her off her game, just a little bit.

His lips twitched—the bastard knew he'd thrown her—but she laughed, delighted with the turn of events. Of the feeling of *fitting* with him again.

With a little start, she realized the others were waiting for her to continue. She cleared her throat. "Right. Moving on. I also want to update the interior a bit—not a lot, actually. It has such a great vibe. But I think we can declutter the back of the bar so you can see more of what's happening in the mirror behind the shelving. And I'd like to add a smaller, free-standing bar over near the stage for when the place is really hopping. I bet that could up your drink income significantly."

"No argument from me," Tyree said. "Show me what you have in mind."

She did, then moved on to how the specific renovation projects would work into the schedule for the show. "The truth is, we could finish easily before the end of the contest, especially as the contest for each guy is spaced out every two weeks."

"But that doesn't work with our plans," Molly added.

"So we'd like to do some work on that smaller bar area you have in the back as well. It wasn't part of the original proposal, and we know it won't be used for the contest, but we hope that providing materials and labor will be incentive."

Jenna and the men exchanged glances. "I think we'll all be just fine with that," Tyree said.

Molly laughed. "We thought you probably would be. There's just one other thing..." She trailed off, her eyes aimed at Spencer. "Andy and I would like to add a bit of whimsy to the show."

"Whimsy?" Reece repeated. "Like what?"

"We want Spencer to be a contestant."

Spencer had just taken a sip of coffee, and now he choked as he tried to swallow. "What? Are you kidding? No way."

"It would be great for the show," Molly urged. "Which ends up benefiting everyone."

"Except I don't—"

"I think it sounds great," Brooke said, shooting him a mischievous smile.

"You do, do you?"

"It would be good for us, too," Jenna said. "Right now, we only have ten contestants invited in. Our goal is twelve guys for each month's contest."

"See?" Brooke said, unable to hide her amusement. "You'd be fabulous up there. And it really would be a fun twist for the show. And, hey, you'd get to strut around shirtless."

"You'd like that?"

"I'm thinking all the women in the bar will like that." She cocked her head, challenging him.

And to her surprise, he met her gaze, nodded, and said, "All right. Looks like I'm running for Mr. February."

Chapter Thirteen

"YOU KNOW why they're doing this, don't you?" Spencer asked Brooke. They were still at Brent's house, though the meeting had broken up.

"What? The Mr. February contest?"

"Don't act innocent," he said, pointing a finger at her. She pretended to bite the end of it, then laughed.

"You said you were okay with it," she said.

"I figured it was better than whatever drama they have in mind otherwise."

She considered that, her eyes widening as she followed his train of thought. "Oh. You think that they're worried about the show since we're getting along." She cocked her head, then smiled at him. "Maybe we should be cold and distant? Or fight a lot? I could throw things. But that wouldn't work since you're so hard headed anyway."

"Watch it," he said, laughing as he hooked an arm around her waist and pulled her into a sideways hug.

She sighed and leaned happily against him. This was nice. Warm and comfortable without any tension.

Well, maybe *some* tension. But it was the good kind. That she hoped to work out later. Together. In bed.

"Daddy!" A little voice carried into the dining room, and Jenna scooped up the girl as she padded in wearing footie pajamas.

"Hey, Faith. Aren't you supposed to be in bed?"

"Where's Daddy?"

"He walked Uncle Tyree out to his car. He'll be right back."

"Uncle Tyree! Can I go say bye-bye?"

"Okay. Off you go." She put the girl down, then glanced up at Reece, who'd been watching the whole encounter, his expression soft. "I'll follow just in case." She passed him on the way, and Brooke saw the way Reece brushed his hand gently across Jenna's belly.

Jenna hadn't said anything, but Brooke had a feeling the other woman was pregnant. Something sweet and soft twisted inside Brooke, and she forced herself not to look at Spencer. That's what she wanted. A house. A family. *Spencer.*

They'd gotten so far off course that she had no idea if they could ever get back. And they definitely couldn't if she didn't tell him the truth about why she'd left.

She just wasn't sure how to dive into that conversation.

Several days later, she still hadn't figured out how to broach the subject, but she also didn't have time to think about it because they were thick in the middle of things at the bar.

For days, they'd been going pretty much non-stop, working from early in the morning until the bar opened. Then they'd camp out at one of the tables and eat lunch while they planned the next day's renovation.

Everything was going great. The stage was gone, and

the replacement was coming along nicely. Brooke didn't have any worries about finishing it on time. That, of course, was the top priority, since it had to be in place by the next show, and she and Spencer were working together with the kind of connection that came from years of reading the other's mind and anticipating needs.

Except they hadn't had years. And that, thought Brooke, boded very well for their future.

He was the best part about the work—and the most frustrating. Because every time they were close, she'd feel the brush of his hand across her back. Or his hip butting against hers as they stood at the bar to go over the plans. He'd brush her hair back behind her ear, the inevitable contact of his fingertips on her cheek driving her a little crazy.

She didn't think he was doing it on purpose, but he was driving her stark raving crazy with need.

He was also, of course, doing it on camera, though they'd gotten so used to the two camera guys hanging unobtrusively in the background that she couldn't say she truly cared about that. Except for the little rush of pleasure when she thought about the fact that those touches would be memorialized on film. They'd be real. Solid. As if capturing them with the camera meant that things would work out between her and Spencer. Silly, she knew, but it gave her a thrill.

But little touches on camera were one thing, bold gestures were something else entirely. So when he came over to her, took her hand, and pulled her close against him, she gasped and swiveled to look for the camera.

"Hey," he said. "Come out with me tonight."

"Tonight? Why?"

It was the wrong question to ask, because all she did

was light a fire under already smoldering embers. He leaned forward, his mouth right at her ear. "Because I want you," he said, then teased her ear with his tongue in the kind of way that had her knees go weak, and made her very grateful for the arm around her waist.

"Spencer," she protested, though not very hard. "We're on camera. Not to mention it's noon. The bar's open to the public now."

"So? All anyone will see is me wanting you." He pulled back, his expression mischievous. "The producers want drama, right?" He traced her lips with his fingertip, and she stifled a moan. "If we're not going to fight, maybe they'll be happy with that old adage—sex sells."

She burst out laughing. "Yeah," she said, "I think we can make them happy."

They were both breathing hard. "So you'll come tonight?"

"We need to work. The contest is in a week and a half."

"It's Saturday night. We won't get any work done here. And all the planning is done. Say yes, Brooke," he urged, lowering his voice. "Please."

It was a simple word, but it shot through her, all of the unspoken implications filling her and making her entire body tingle with desire.

"Come on," he pressed. "Say yes."

She was about to say that very thing when she glanced toward the door—and saw her father standing right inside the bar.

"Shit." He might as well have poured ice water all over her. Not only did she not want to see her dad, but his presence only reminded her of the truth she needed to tell Spencer. "I'll be right back."

To her relief, Spencer didn't try to stop her or come

with her. "What are you doing here?" she asked when she reached her father.

"I see you didn't pay any attention to our talk the other day."

"Nice to know you don't need glasses, Daddy. You see just fine."

He pinched the bridge of his nose. "If you insist on following this path, at least do it with dignity."

Her brows lifted. "Excuse me?"

"I'll accept that this is your career of choice—the remodeling work, I mean. You clearly have a knack for it, and you have a solid reputation in the community."

She crossed her arms over her chest. "You've been checking up on me. Gee, I'm flattered."

"I'm offering to capitalize *The Business Plan*. Your business. Not this ridiculous show. Leave the show to Mr. Dean. You go back to your work, and I'll make sure you have enough capital to allow you to take on larger and more prestigious projects. The same result you're looking for with this show, isn't it?"

It was, but she wasn't going to admit that out loud.

"Why?"

"I already told you. I don't want you in bed—literally or metaphorically—with that man. He's bad news. Did you ask him about his financial issues? You do not need to attach your cart to that horse. Sooner or later, he's going to disappoint you."

Anger bubbled inside her. She wanted to tell him to go to hell. That this wasn't about her—it was about him not getting his own way. About her being with Spencer again, despite her father jumping through every hoop imaginable.

She wanted to say all of that. But she held herself in

check. Instead, all she said was, "Daddy, I think it's time for you to go."

Then she turned her back on him and walked toward Spencer, hoping to God that she wouldn't hyperventilate and pass out on the way.

"Is he still there?" she asked.

"Sending me daggers with his eyes," Spencer confirmed.

"Kiss me."

His eyes went wide.

"Dammit, Spencer, kiss me."

He did, and it was exactly the kind of kiss she craved. A kiss with tongue and teeth that ricocheted through her, making her ache with need. Hard and wild and demanding and *claiming*. That was the key. She wanted him to claim her. To own her. To prove to her, her father, everyone that she was his again, even if she really wasn't. Not yet.

But, dammit, she wanted to be.

When they broke apart, they were both breathing hard. "Tonight," she said. "When and where?"

His grin was mischievous as he handed her a folded slip of paper. "I wrote it down for you. Take an Uber. You won't need your car. And yes," he said, as she unfolded the paper, "it's a test."

Meet me where we first kissed. 7pm.

She looked back up at him and grinned. "I'll be there by six forty-five."

Chapter Fourteen

AT ALMOST EIGHT hundred feet above sea level, Mount Bonnell stood as the highest point in Austin, and pretty much everyone in the city had been there at one time or another to see the view of the city, Lake Austin, and the surrounding hills.

Spencer had been coming there since he was a kid. He'd climb the one hundred and two steps all the way to the top, then circumvent the pretty, paved picnic area for the rougher wilderness beyond. He'd find a good, flat spot in the dirt and scrub, then put down a blanket, sit, and watch the world move along below him.

When he got older and began thinking about reno-vating homes, he'd take a notebook and sketch out his plans.

The place had always held a magical quality to him, and even though he was rarely alone there, he liked to think of it as his own.

Which was why when he brought Brooke there the evening of the second day he'd known her, he'd been as jumpy as if he'd sat in a pile of fire ants. He'd met her only twenty-four hours before, and yet he'd taken her out after he'd repaired her tire, and that non-date had been about the most perfect evening he'd spent with a woman.

He'd been smitten—no other word for it. And though he hadn't kissed her that night, it had been all he'd thought about until the next evening when she joined him on this iconic outcropping.

That was then. But things hadn't changed much, because having Brooke beside him at the park was still all he could think about. And even though it was barely six forty-five, he kept turning back to the stairs to see if she was coming.

· And then, like a miracle, there she was.

She stood on the landing at the top of the stairs, the stunning spread of sky and trees a poor backdrop to her beauty. She wore jeans and a T-shirt and looked as sexy as he'd ever seen her.

Frowning, she cupped her hand at her forehead as she glanced around, obviously searching for him. He waited a second—stupid, but he liked knowing that she was seeking him out. Then he stepped into her view, and was rewarded with a smile as bright as sunshine.

"Hey," she said. "Fancy meeting you here."

"Come on," he said, holding out his hand, and then leading her away from the stairs to a nearby dirt path. They followed it a bit, then pushed their way through some juniper branches to a secluded section he'd found when he'd walked the area upon arriving.

"This is perfect," she said, looking at the blanket he'd spread over the rocks and dirt. A few feet ahead, the hill seemed to fall away below them. And though he wasn't about to let her get too close to the edge, even when they were seated, they had a view of the river. And, soon, they'd have a view of an amazing sunset.

He put his arm around her, and she leaned against him, her sigh sounding like a mix of both pleasure and relief.

"You okay?"

She tilted her head so that she could smile at him. "I am now."

He brushed a quick kiss over her lips, making her laugh and murmur, "Tickles."

He chuckled. "Should I shave?"

"Hell no. You're perfect."

The words warmed him, but once again, he was catching that vibe. As if something wasn't quite right. And as much as he hated thinking it, he was afraid it might be him. "Brooke, what's wrong?"

This time when she looked at him, she was scowling. "That obvious?"

"Maybe I just know you well."

"You do," she said. "Even after all this time. This is like a miracle to me. That we're back together. That maybe if we don't screw it up, we'll get a happily ever after."

Her words sent rocket flares of joy careening through him. *He'd* been thinking along that way—hell, yeah, he had—but he hadn't been certain that she had. And this was the first time either of them had spoken concretely about a future.

"I can see why that would make you upset," he said, his voice deadpan.

As he'd hoped, she laughed. "Yeah, well, you forgot about the monkey in our wrench."

He felt the smile tug at his lips. "Did I?"

"It pisses me off that my dad keeps poking and poking."

"Ah." He leaned back, his hands behind him for support. He should have realized that the encounter with her dad wouldn't simply blow over. "What did he want earlier?"

"Oh, only for me to quit the show and get away from you. And as incentive, he said that he'd underwrite my entire business so that I can take on bigger, more prestigious jobs."

He felt his mouth go a little dry. "Not a bad offer."

She rolled her eyes. "It's a terrible offer. Be in business with my dad? Especially if it meant that you weren't in the picture?"

"I know. But he loves you. He wants to help you."

Her blue eyes went as hard as flint. "What he wants is you out of my life, and this time he's using my business as leverage."

His radar tingled. "This time?"

She nodded, suddenly looking much younger than her twenty-eight years. "I need to tell you something," she whispered. "You might hate me—I won't blame you if you do. But the thought of losing you again terrifies me." A thick tear dropped from her lashes to the blanket as another trailed down the side of her nose.

Dread raced up his spine. He wanted to reassure her that everything would be fine, but all he could manage to say was, "Tell me."

"It was my father," she said, her words slow and measured.

"Your father? What was?"

"Our wedding. When I met you in the garden and told

you I couldn't go through with it." She licked her lips. "I didn't want to—oh, God, I so didn't want to."

He wanted to shout. To shake her and ask why she'd done that to him—*to them*—if she hadn't wanted to. But that was the story she was telling, and his hurt and anger wouldn't make it easier for either of them.

He kept silent, and she pressed on, watching him as she spoke. He could see the exhaustion—and the relief—in her face as the words flowed. It was as if she'd been holding it all in behind a dam and was finally allowed to let it all slip out, the whole story about the promise her father had made about clemency for Richie. And the terrible choice that Brooke had been forced to make.

He said nothing until she finished, then sat up and put his head down on his knees, his arms curled around his legs, shutting out the world. *Her father.*

Her goddamn father had saved his brother. "He'd had the power," he said finally, turning his head to look at her. "Your dad held my brother's life in his hands. And the fucker used that power to play puppet master and pull all three of our strings."

"I know," she said. "Believe me, I know."

"You should have told me. You should have trusted me enough to come to me with that. If not before, then at least after the Governor granted clemency."

"I wanted to—hell, I planned to. But then my dad told me that he'd found out about your record." She licked her lips. "All the stuff from after Richie was arrested, when you said you went off the rails." She swallowed audibly. "He said he was going to tell your producer, and it would be a scandal on social media, and they'd yank the show."

"Christ." He scrubbed his hands over his face. "You should have told me."

"That's the point. If I'd told you he would have held all that stuff over you. He would have destroyed you. Don't pretend I'm wrong. You didn't exactly advertise your past to the producers. I was there, remember? You kept telling me over and over that you had to come across as a guy folks related to."

"And people don't relate to kids from shit neighborhoods who have to scrape by," he retorted, his already on-edge temper flaring. "Who go a little nuts when their brother ends up on death row. Who skirt up against gangs and fight like hell not to get sucked all the way in. No, I guess most people don't relate to that."

She leaned forward and pressed a hand to his knee. "That's not what I mean, and you know it."

"No, you were afraid I'd lose the show, and we couldn't have that." He was talking out his ass, and he knew it. Anger and pain and years of regret fueling harsh words that he wanted to call back even as he spoke them. "A construction worker from the east side wasn't good enough for you."

Her palm flew out and struck him hard against the cheek.

"Fuck you, Spencer Dean. *Fuck. You.*" Tears glistened on her lashes. "I was right beside you for years before that show was even a twinkle in your eye, but when it did spark, you wanted it, and don't you dare deny that, because *I* know. I know because I'm the one you told. And I was faced with a horrible, awful Hobson's choice, and I did what I thought was right, dammit."

"You protected me."

"Yes." She sniffled, then wiped her nose on her sleeve.

"You shouldn't be the one protecting me. I should be protecting you."

Her laugh bubbled out, the sound rough with tears. "Oh my God, what are you? A Neanderthal?"

"Where you were concerned, yeah, I guess I was."

He saw a sparkle in her eyes, and the hint of a smile touch her lips.

"I should have been there," he continued, taking her hand, the connection electric. "You shouldn't have had to deal with all of that alone."

"Nice in theory," she said, as he stroked the back of her hand with his thumb. "Under the circumstances that would have been a little hard in practice." She met his eyes, her lips slightly parted, her breath coming hard.

"I'm sorry," he said, and though he wanted to say more, he couldn't. Not yet. He didn't need the words, he needed *her*. And so he pulled her to him, settling her on his lap, and lowering his mouth to hers. She met him greedily, teeth clashing, mouths searching, hands groping. He couldn't get enough of her. He wanted to claim her—*had* to claim her. Had to let her and her father and the whole damn world know that she was his, goddammit.

Roughly, he pulled her down until they were both on the ground, Brooke soft and yielding beneath him. His knee was between her legs, and he was as hard as stone. Her hands tightened in his hair, pulling him more firmly against her.

He deepened the kiss, losing himself to the feel of her and the fantasy that, somehow, this moment could fix everything. As if there was magic in it, and if he could simply kiss her long enough or well enough, he'd never lose her again.

"Please," she said, her hands going to his fly.

He groaned and almost came right then—and in the same moment, his senses returned. They were on a fucking hill, in a city park. And as gorgeous as the sunset might be, there was nothing romantic about taking her in the dirt like a damned teenager with hormones on overdrive.

"How much do you want to see the sunset?"

"What?" Her voice was heavy, lost in a sensual haze.

"Leave now, we miss the sunset. Your choice."

"Screw the sunset," she said, making his heart swell. "Take me home."

Chapter Fifteen

AS FAR AS Brooke was concerned, riding on the back of a Harley was about as potent an aphrodisiac as anything ever invented. And as for the uses of vibrators in foreplay...

Well, a motorcycle put them all to shame.

Which explained why the moment she and Spencer were through the front door of her small, comfortable house, she had him up against the wall, her arms around his neck, and her crotch grinding against his thigh. Shameless, maybe, but she knew what she wanted. *Him.*

It had, frankly, been too damn long.

"Well, hello to you, too," he said, but she was in no mood for teasing, so she shut him up with a kiss.

Spencer, to his credit, got the message right away. One of his hands slid down to cup her ass, then the other moved up her back underneath her T-shirt, his palm warm against her skin.

"Off," she begged. "Please, pull it off."

He knew what she meant, and his hands moved just long enough to grab the hem of her shirt and pull upwards, tugging it over her head and tossing it carelessly on the floor. She reached back, unfastened her bra, and wriggled out of it.

Then she took Spencer's hands and pressed them over her breasts, sighing with pleasure when he groaned in delight. "Do you have any idea how much I adore your hands?" she asked.

"At least as much as I adore every inch of you."

"Oh, sure. Show me up." She started to laugh, but the sound turned into a strangled gasp when he used his thumbs and forefingers to pinch her nipples, then capture her mouth with a hard, demanding kiss.

She opened to him, drinking in the masculine taste of him, melting under the raw sensation of his beard against her lips, her cheek, her chin. Most of all, losing herself to the heady pleasure of knowing that he was hers. To tease and touch and take.

He pulled back, dragging his teeth over her lower lip as he broke the kiss. She whimpered in protest, but he silenced her with as simple command to, "Trust me."

Since she did, she closed her eyes and let her head fall back, losing herself to both the sensation of his touch and to the wonderful, mind-blowing knowledge that the universe had turned right-side up, and they were truly together again.

With a wicked, torturous slowness, he kissed his way down her neck, over her shoulder, and then on to her breast. She expected him to go lower, but he paused there, his tongue taking over for his hand as he sucked and teased her nipple, making threads of electric pleasure cut through her like lightning in a thunderstorm.

As his mouth performed that magic feat, his fingers explored further south, moving lower over her abdomen and leaving her skin hot and tingling in the wake of his insistent touch.

While his tongue and teeth teased her nipple, his fingers attacked her jeans, opening the button with expert skill. He tugged the zipper down, then slid his flattened hand into her skinny jeans, so tight that once he'd cupped her sex, he could only move a finger. But those movements were made with all the skill of an expert.

His fingertip teased her clit as his mouth ravaged her breast, and his other hand shifted up to hold her tight around the waist, keeping her steady as the heat of rising passion spun and whirled inside her, a hot wire of pleasure running from her nipple to her clit.

She was close, so very close, and though she knew he wanted her to go over, she didn't want that. Not yet.

She had something else in mind.

"Wait," she said, her voice raw with pleasure, her head light with need. "I want you inside me. Now. Fast and hard. Please, Spencer, help me get out of these damn jeans."

"Whatever the lady wants," he said, his hands moving with lightning speed to her hips to tug the jeans down.

Since it was May, she'd been wearing sandals, and she kicked those off easily as her own fingers found his fly and began going to work on the button and zipper.

He moved to help, starting to pull them down, but she stayed his hand. "No. You stay dressed. Just me. Naked for you."

He lifted a brow. "I like a woman who takes control."

She almost laughed out loud. "Good," she said, then kissed him hard before she eased back to the small table onto which she tossed her mail. He must have seen her purpose reflected on her face, because he flashed a wicked grin, then took her by the waist and lifted her.

And then, once she was seated, he put his hands on her knees, spread her legs, and dropped down to kneel in front of her.

That, frankly, wasn't what she'd had in mind. She wanted it hard. She wanted him to fill her, to pound himself inside her. To shake the table and make the pictures rattle on the wall.

But when his beard scraped her inner thighs, and he slowly stroked his tongue over the length of her sex, she had to concede that his plan had merit, too.

His tongue played her expertly, and she arched back, her hands clutching the edge of the table, her breath coming in staccato bursts as the familiar pressure built inside her, a warning of a coming explosion.

"No," she whispered, wanting the explosion, but also wanting more. "Spencer, here." Her fingers twined in his hair, and she tugged him up. "I need you inside me."

She saw the raw heat flare in his eyes, and knew she had him. And when he eased his cock out of his open jeans and moved toward her, she inched to the edge of the table, spreading her legs even wider in invitation. Needing him. Needing *them.*

"I don't have a condom," he said, his voice raw.

"It's okay. I'm on birth control. *Please,*" she added. "Don't stop."

"Never," he promised, and to her relief, he took her fast. His hands cupped her ass, holding her steady as he eased into her, slowly at first and then with deep, powerful thrusts that filled her to the core. Again and again they rocked together, their bodies joined as one as she clutched him around the neck, holding tight and riding hard.

She felt his body stiffen when he was close, then had confirmation when his voice rasped in her ear, telling her to come with him. To go over. To please, dammit, come with him.

And then, as he exploded inside her, she felt her own body let go, and she shattered into a million pieces, tied to earth by Spencer's strong arms that kept her tethered.

After, she was limp as a rag, but she managed to hook her legs around his waist and her arms around his neck as he carried her to the bed. There, she snuggled close, her back against Spencer's body, her rear tucked in perfectly against his hips. He had one arm around her and was holding her close, the steady rhythm of his breathing soothing her. She felt warm and safe ... and, despite the lingering pleasure, she also felt worried.

"Spence?"

"Hmm."

"This thing with my dad—there's nothing he can do about Richie since the Governor can't take back clemency once he's granted it. But if he decides to release all that stuff about your record now that we're seeing each other again, will it hurt you?"

She could feel him stiffen and wished that she'd waited until morning. Then he propped himself up on his elbow and urged her to turn around and face him. "I am what I am, and it's not as if keeping it a secret will change that. But no, I don't think it would matter. Not for the show, if that's what you mean. Just more fodder for the social media machine."

She nodded, at first accepting the answer, pleased that her father's machinations wouldn't get him kicked off the show or banned from doing *Mansion Makeover*, a show he'd told her about one afternoon at The Fix. "I want to bring our place back to life," he'd said, and she'd told him that she could think of no one better to do that.

But as she lay there in the cradle of his arms, she couldn't help but wonder about his tone. *I am what I am.*

She played the words over in her head, then closed her eyes, finally understanding the pain and frustration she'd heard in his voice. "You are, you know," she whispered.

"What's that?"

"You are what you are. You're talented and kind and smart and sexy as hell. And I—"

"Brooke." Her name was sharp and spoken like an order.

She rolled over to face him.

"It's okay," he said. "I know where I come from, and it's a long way from your father's world."

"Spencer," she began, but then paused. She knew damn well that he'd grown up being painfully aware of his background. A scholarship kid in a ritzy school. The kid brother of a convicted killer. The child of a father who had to scrape to keep a roof over their heads.

She also knew that the difference in their social statuses had bothered him. But they'd never bothered her, dammit. And he should know that. They'd talked about it over and over before their aborted wedding—but maybe he'd believed that was why she'd walked all those years ago.

If so, now he should know better.

Besides, he'd made something of himself, so whatever his issues with his past, that's exactly what they were. *Past.*

Surely that wasn't what she was hearing in his voice now. Spencer knew better than anyone that he'd pulled himself up.

Which meant that this was about what her father saw, and Judge Hamlin wasn't a man inclined to look beyond the barest of facts where his little girl was concerned. So, yeah, Spencer had every right to be irritated.

"What?" he pressed, and she realized she'd gotten lost in her thoughts.

"Nothing." She ran her hand along his beard, feeling his whiskers rub against her palm. "Just that I love you." She paused, realizing what she'd said. "Oh—Spencer, I—"

"Didn't mean it?" She heard the forced humor in his voice.

"*No*," she said fiercely, hoping like hell that he wasn't going to pat her on the head and tell her that her feelings were sweet but unreturned. "I meant it. I *mean* it. But I hadn't intended to say it."

She licked her lips. "It's okay if you don't feel the same. I mean, I never really stopped loving you. I just had to get to know you again. You—" She swallowed, her voice breaking on a sob. "You hated me for a while. That's a lot to get past."

"It is," he said gently. Then he kissed her, soft and sweet and so full of love that it made her feel like the most powerful, beautiful woman in the world. "And I love you, too."

She closed her eyes on a sigh. "Thank God," she said. "It would suck to be alone in this."

They both laughed, and he rolled over, pulling her on top of him. She straddled him, then leaned in for a kiss. "Can I ask you something?"

"Anything."

"Why are you doing the show, really?"

"Because of you."

She blushed with pleasure. "Liar."

He chuckled, then pulled her down so that they were skin to skin, her head nestled under his chin. "Not at first,

I'll admit that. But now—even if I had to give up the Drysdale Mansion, I'd stay on the show."

"So it's all worked out? You'll end up with ownership of the house after *Mansion Makeover* airs?"

"Am I a brilliant negotiator, or what?"

"I'm impressed," she admitted, then drew in a breath, thinking.

"What?"

"Well, I—oh, hell. Did you talk to an attorney before you signed the papers?"

"An attorney? Well, Gregory looked over the series contract. That's my agent. And Amanda's doing the real estate deal. Why would I—"

"Because it would suck if the IRS got the mansion," she blurted, rolling over and sitting up as she spoke.

His brow furrowed. "It would," he agreed. "Do you know something I don't?"

"I thought—I mean, Daddy suggested... *Oh*. He was bullshitting again."

"What did he say?"

She waved her hands, annoyed with her father anew for making her worry about Spencer's solvency. "I don't remember exactly. Tax problems and money laundering allegations. All sorts of craziness."

"And all true," Spencer said, his voice as hard as his features. "Just not me."

"Oh." She crossed her legs and pulled the sheet up. "Color me confused."

He pushed himself up to a sitting position, his back to the headboard. "You still see much of Brian?"

The unexpected question hit her with the force of an avalanche. Her chest tightened, and her throat closed up. She clutched the sheet tight in her fists and forced herself to breathe normally. "No. We—um—don't really talk anymore." *There.* The truth. Some of it, anyway. And at least her voice sounded normal.

"Consider yourself lucky. Rat bastard screwed me."

Me, too. The thought came unbidden, but she didn't voice it. Instead, she asked, "What happened?"

"What happened is I hired Brian as my financial advisor and he screwed me nine ways to Sunday. It was a huge fucking mess there for a while, but my credit's clear now. My bank account, however, is pretty damn empty."

"My God."

"Who would have believed our boy Brian could be such a shit, right?"

She licked her lips, but didn't answer. She could believe it. Boy, could she ever.

"Did you go to the cops?"

He nodded. "I did—but I'll be honest. It was a close call. Brian's damn lucky to have any bones in his face."

She swallowed, quite certain that wasn't meant as a figure of speech. "Why didn't you?"

One shoulder rose and fell as he made a derisive noise in the back of his throat. "Because it was on me, too. I trusted him. Gave him way too much control. And I didn't pay attention. I'll toss the law at him under those circumstances, but since I was negligent, too, he got to keep his face. But damn, do I wish I had another excuse to put the fucker in the ground."

Her chest tightened. She knew damn well that if he ever found out the truth, *she'd* be that excuse.

"My turn, Angel," he said, his voice laced with gentleness. "What happened to you?"

Her blood turned to ice. "What do you mean?"

"You can tell me it's none of my business if you want

to, but if we're going to keep sleeping together, then I think maybe it is. Am I right?"

She studied her fingernails.

"It's okay." He laid his hand over hers. "I'm not going to push. But if someone hurt—"

"I was roofied." She looked up to see pure rage burning in his eyes, seeping into his skin, so thick it seemed to come off him in waves.

He pulled his hand back, then clenched it into a fist so tight that when he relaxed, she saw the indentions in his palms. "Who?"

One word, and yet it held all of her pain. And the promise of painful retribution.

She thought of Brian. Of what Spencer had just told her. "I—I don't know."

His brows rose.

"I was at a party," she lied. "There was a guy and he was chatting me up. Then he got me a drink and—"

She pressed her lips together but kept her eyes wide open to fight back the tears. Stupid, foolish tears after all this time.

"Did he tie you up? I saw how you looked at the bed," he added hurriedly. "In the hotel."

She shook her head. "No. At least, I don't think so. He didn't—hurt me."

"The hell he didn't."

She laughed mirthlessly. "Well, you know what I mean. I didn't have cuts or bruises. And I didn't catch anything."

"He raped you."

"Yes." He stole her control. Violated her trust. Destroyed a friendship.

For a moment, Spencer simply breathed, and she saw

the pain in his eyes along with the hint of tears. And seeing it, she almost lost her shit all over again.

"I'm okay now," she said, taking his hand, giving him back the comfort that seeing his anger and pain had given her. "Truly."

"No," he said gently, taking her chin and tilting her head up to look at him. "You're not. But I'd like to help. Is there anything I can do to make it better?"

"You already do," she said honestly, her chest swelling from the tenderness in his eyes. "But maybe right now you could kiss me."

Something like regret flickered in his eyes. "I don't think this is the kind of thing I can kiss and make better. But, Angel," he added, pulling her close, "I'm definitely willing to try."

Chapter Sixteen

"THAT STAGE IS a work of serious genius," Reece said, holding up a beer in toast.

"Hear, hear!" Brent added, clinking glasses with Tyree, who was starting his second bottle.

"Are we allowed to do this?" Cameron asked. "I mean, it's after two." He shot a glance toward Tyree. "And you once told me you'd fire my ass if I sold a drop of liquor after closing."

As soon as he finished speaking, he winced, then tilted his head toward Casper, the cameraman, as if Cameron had made a major faux pas on tape.

Casper, however, appeared completely uninterested. That wasn't his name, of course. But on the second day of filming, Mina had announced that since they weren't supposed to know either cameraman's real name—and since the men were supposed to be invisible to all of them—they'd name them appropriately. Thus, the shorter cameraman was Casper and his taller counterpart was Nick.

"Nick?" Cam had asked, and Mina had rolled her eyes.

"As in Nearly Headless? A ghost, right? Like invisible. Fades away."

Cam, Brooke noticed, was still eyeing the beer suspiciously. Tyree, however, was unconcerned. On the contrary, a wide, delighted grin split his face. "And that's why my boy here is going to be getting that weekend assistant manager gig," Tyree said, directing the comment to Spencer and Brooke.

Then he waved his hand, indicating the spread of beer and liquor covering the desk in his office. "But this, my law-abiding young friend, is my own private stash. No sale, no problem. But don't drive home."

Cameron laughed, obviously relieved. "Fair enough."

Mina, who was sitting on the desk, pushed out her foot and bumped Cam's chair. "You are way too law-abiding."

"Just being careful," Cam protested, but he looked down immediately, and not for the first time Brooke wondered if he'd ever get up the nerve to tell Mina how he felt. Maybe if he downed a couple more beers...

It was after hours on Sunday, and the impromptu party was in celebration of the completion of the sectional stage. "I am completely willing to take a bow," Spencer said. "And I can do it with complete and total humbleness since it wasn't my brilliance that designed the thing. That would be the lovely Brooke Hamlin."

"Thank you, thank you," she said, taking a bow as they all applauded. "I honestly can't believe the contest is only a few days away."

Tyree nodded. "It's amazing how much you two have gotten done."

"Not just us," Brooke said. "You guys and your staff all helped." In the interest of the show, they'd decided to forego hiring laborers when they needed an extra pair of hands. Instead, when Brooke or Spencer needed help, management or one of the waiters or kitchen staff kicked in. And so far, they hadn't needed to pull in outside contractors like plumbers or electricians.

"We did," Brent agreed. "But you two still make a great team."

"Yeah," Spence said, hooking his arm around Brooke and pulling her in for a quick kiss, "we do."

"I think you have a pretty good shot on Wednesday," Jenna said to Spencer. She was drinking club soda with lime, and took a long sip before continuing. "I saw more than a few of our lunchtime regulars watching you work the last few days."

"Can't blame them. He looks hot in a T-shirt," Brooke said. They'd decided to work through the lunch hour in order to keep the show interesting by having customers in the place. "Especially with the sleeves rolled up to show off his ink."

"Which is excellent, by the way," Reece said, raising his glass in another toast. Considering the beauty and intricacy of his own tats, Brooke figured that was high praise.

"Right back at you," Spence said.

"I figure you'll score some points with the tats," Mina said.

"Wait." Brent frowned. "Wednesday? Points?"

"That's right," Jenna said. "You missed that conversation. Spencer's competing for Mr. February."

Brent laughed out loud. "Oh, man. Better you than me, buddy."

"Please. You are so getting on that stage one of these days," Jenna countered.

"Hell, yes, he is," Reece agreed.

Brent, however, merely pointed a finger at both of

them and shook his head before turning to Spencer. "Good luck with that."

"Hey," Spence said. "I'm gonna own that shit." He flexed his muscles, and they all cracked up.

"Well, my money's on you," Brooke said.

"Mine's on Cam," Mina said. "Come on, Cameron. You know you want to."

"The hell I do."

"You should," she pressed. "We're still one guy short."

Tyree frowned. "Are we?"

Jenna nodded. "We don't have a hard rule that it has to be twelve contestants for each slot, so I wouldn't say we're *short*. We did manage to get twelve. But then one guy had to drop out. He got called out of town on business."

"See?" Mina pressed.

"Could he do it?" Brent asked. "I thought we were having local celebrities narrow down the applications to the final twelve."

Jenna lifted a shoulder. "I could get his application to them on Monday. I know they'd say yes."

"Um, hello. Right here."

Mina started to say something, but Brent pointed a finger to hush her. "If Cam wants to enter, he can tell Jenna later."

"Fine." Mina lifted her hands in surrender.

"I've had way too many of these," Brooke said. "I'm going to the ladies room. Back in a sec."

She was still thinking about the expression on Cam's face when she left the restroom a few minutes later. Maybe he would enter. She hoped he did. He was damn sure good-looking enough. True, he had a sweet, shy streak that made him seem younger than his years. But toss a little confidence his way, and—

"Oh!" She jumped, then realized that the hard body she'd walked into in the dark was Spencer.

"I was looking for you." Heat infused his voice.

"Were you? How interesting."

"Mmm." He pressed her up against the wall, caging her in. "Wasn't that long ago I held you like this with a completely different motive."

"My, how things changed." She hooked her arms around his waist then rose up on her toes to kiss him. "Did you find me out here for a tryst?"

"Actually, I have news. The tryst is just a perk."

"News?" She heard the excitement in his voice. "Spencer? What's going on?"

"I got an email from Richie's attorney."

Brooke's heart started to beat double-time. "This late? That can't be good."

"Actually, it is. She said she was working late on his case and realized she hadn't given me a heads-up."

"His case? I thought he was out of appeals."

"He's up for parole." Spencer's voice was tight with hope.

"What? That's incredible."

"I know. He's already had his interview."

"When will he hear if parole is granted?"

"We're not sure." He ran his fingers through his hair. "Fifteen years, Brooke. It's forever, but if he can get out now, he can still make a real life."

"This is amazing news," she said, clutching his hand. "And even if he doesn't make it this time, he's in the rotation, right? So he'll come up again with another chance. They don't always grant the first time."

"I know. I need to call his attorney. I'll do that in the morning. Find out all I can."

"In the meantime, we'll send Richie all our good thoughts."

"Hell, yes." He looked into her eyes, his filled with love and hope and vulnerability. "And in the meantime, I'm also taking a kiss for good luck."

"You don't have to take it," she began. "I'll give—"

But she didn't finish. His mouth closed over hers, gentle at first, but then hard and demanding, as if he could foist his will on the parole board through her. His fingers twined in her hair, tilting her head back, and his other hand went around her waist, pulling her to him so that she felt his erection straining against his jeans.

Her knees were weak, her body tingling, and she clung to him, as desperate for him as he was for her.

A low wolf whistle brought her back to her senses, and she leaped back, banging her elbow against the wall.

Reece chuckled. "You might want to think about getting a room. Before Casper decides to turn on his camera."

Spencer caught her eye and grinned. "You into exhibitionism?"

"Really not."

He shot a quick salute to Reece, who was laughing his ass off. "I think that's our cue to leave. Catch you in the morning. I'm taking this party home."

Chapter Seventeen

SPENCER DROVE BROOKE'S CAR, and as far as he was concerned, it was the longest ride anywhere. He'd made the journey with his hand on her bare thigh, thanking God and the universe that she'd worn a simple cotton skirt tonight, and not the jeans she wore when they were knee-deep in lumber and paint.

He'd tried once during the drive to ease his hand even higher up that firm thigh. To move slowly, inch by delicious inch, until he reached the band of her panties. And then he'd fully intended to slip his finger under the smooth satin and stroke her waxed pussy until she pressed her hands hard against the roof of the car, arched her body up, and cried his name while surrendering to one hell of a massive orgasm.

As far as he was concerned, that was an A-one fantasy. But a fantasy it had remained, because at the first sign that he was inching his fingers toward heaven, Brooke had smacked her own hand on top of his, stalling his progress.

"If you think that I'm going to risk death on these city

streets just so you can cop a feel, you are very sadly mistaken."

It wasn't the most romantic sentiment, but he took her point. And he'd contented himself with simply caressing her thigh and telling her in very specific detail how he intended to fuck her so hard when they got home that she was going to scream for mercy.

To his satisfaction, she'd closed her eyes and surrendered to his comparatively tame touch. And as for the effect of his words ... well, from the way she bit her lower lip and the prominence of her nipples against her cotton blouse, he was certain he'd hit the mark.

Now, he turned into her driveway and killed the engine. *Finally*, they'd arrived.

He glanced sideways at her. "You know you're a cruel woman."

She didn't open her eyes, but the corners of her mouth lifted in a smile. "Maybe it wasn't really about car safety. Maybe I just like tormenting you."

"Oh, no. We both know who was tormenting who."

She turned her head and peered at him through narrowed eyes. "Is that so?"

"You're wet, Angel. Don't even try to deny it."

"You think?"

"I'm certain of it."

Her eyes danced with mirth. "I guess there's only one way for you to find out if you're right." She lifted his hand off her thigh, then drew his forefinger into her mouth, laving it with her tongue. "Why don't you check and see?"

His cock twitched in response to her teasing tone as much as to the sensual invitation that he eagerly accepted. Moving slowly, he did in the driveway what he'd been thinking about ever since they left the bar. He eased his hand up her skirt to her panty line, then slipped his finger under the soft material.

He heard her gasp as he stroked her, her sex smooth and so damn slick with desire that he felt himself grow harder still, just from the evidence of how much she wanted him.

"Inside," he said, the word bursting out with the force of his desire. He started to push open his door. "Now."

"Wait." She reached over, her hand on his thigh stilling him. "Stay."

He tilted his head, studying her. "Stay?"

She nodded, and his brows lifted.

"What exactly do you want?"

"You know," she said.

"You want me to touch you?"

"Yes." Her voice was like breath.

"You want me to make you come?"

"God, yes."

He looked pointedly around. "Could have sworn you said you weren't into exhibitionism."

She reached for his hand, then slid it back inside her panties, making a whimpering sound as she did. "Maybe I'm desperate. Maybe the thought tempted me as we drove home."

"Interesting."

"And it's dark. And there aren't any streetlights, and barely any light from my front porch. And it's after two in the morning."

"My Angel has a bit of the devil in her."

"And if she does?" With a flick of a lever, she dropped her seat back, putting her almost flat on her back beside him. "What are you prepared to do about that?"

He hooked a finger under the hem of her shirt. "Oh, I

think I can come up with something." He tugged up her shirt, then with equal deftness, tugged down her bra, so that her breasts spilled out of the cups.

"Mostly, I want to watch you," he said as he slipped his hand back inside her panties. "The way the dim light from the porch dances on your skin. The way your skin prickles as I stroke you. The way your nipples tighten when I brush the tip of my tongue over them," which he did right then in demonstration.

As he'd anticipated, she drew in a shuddering breath that set her entire body trembling. A trembling that only increased when he teased small circles around her clit, taking her close, but never quite over.

"I want to watch," he repeated. "And I want you to beg."

"Please." Her voice was a whimper. "Spencer, please."

"What do you want?"

"You. This. Make me come." She turned her head and opened her eyes. "Please make me come for you."

Her words sank straight to his cock, hardening it like steel. "Come for me, Angel," he murmured as he teased her pussy. "I want to feel you explode. I want to watch you break apart. I want to see you shatter. And I want to know that I was the one who took you there."

And then, as if his command had been the final piece of a puzzle, she arched up, crying out his name as her hand squeezed his with bone crushing strength. Then, when her trembling had stopped and her breath came easy, she turned to him, her features soft and a satisfied smile playing at her mouth. "Your turn," she murmured. And in that moment, he felt a rush of tenderness that was at least as potent as his desire.

"Damn right it is. But I think I'll take my turn inside.

I'm not sure this little car would take the kind of rocking that what I have in mind would put it through."

She laughed. "In that case, let's hurry."

He didn't argue, and they were at the door and inside in less than a minute. There was a coatrack by the small table in the hallway, and she glanced at it, then back at him.

"What?" he asked as she moved to pull off a black, silk scarf.

"You had scarves tied to bed posts when you took me to the hotel." She pressed her lips together, then continued. "Is that—is that something you'd like?"

Hell yes.

He tilted his head. "Is it something you want?"

"With you?" She drew in a breath and nodded. "Yes."

He chuckled. "Well, I'm damn sure not letting anybody else tie you up. But only if you're sure."

She nodded, though she looked a little hesitant. "I trust you, Spence," she said, her eyes locked on his. "I'm sure."

BONDAGE WASN'T TERRIFYING, Brooke thought. It was sensual, exciting, and deliciously exhilarating.

Of course, the key to that assessment was Spencer. Because if anyone else had rummaged in her top dresser drawer for more scarves and then told her that he was going to tie her down and have his way with her—well, she would have either passed out or run like the wind.

With Spencer, she'd trembled. But it had been a good feeling. Anticipation rather than apprehension.

And when he'd told her to strip for him, she'd done so slowly, knowing that his eyes were on her, and that with each bit of skin she exposed, she was driving him a little bit crazy.

Once she was naked, he'd told her to get on the bed, where the four scarves were tied to the head and footboard of her antique, wrought-iron bedframe. She'd hesitated for just an instant, and he'd kissed her bare shoulder and whispered, "Pumpernickel."

The word was so absurd that she'd laughed, but he told her he was serious. That was the word to use if she freaked out. Say that, and he'd have her loose in a heartbeat.

She believed him, and that sudden rush of absolute trust wiped away the tendrils of fear. She'd climbed on the bed and let him tie down her wrists and ankles.

Once bound, she'd closed her eyes, assessing how she felt, and was surprised to realize that the dominant emotion was anticipation. She didn't know what was coming next—not exactly, anyway—and she knew perfectly well that she was tied fast to the bed—and yet her heart pounded with a wild excitement and her body burned with need. Her breasts felt heavy, as if begging to be touched. Her legs were wide, leaving her exposed, and the thought that Spencer would see her open and ready for him didn't make her shy. On the contrary, she felt oddly powerful.

Yeah. Definitely exhilarating.

And wonderful, too. Because after Brian, any movie or book with any sort of bondage scene had made her stomach curdle. And, honestly, she knew that hadn't really changed. Because it wasn't the idea of being tied down that she was now open to. It was the idea of being tied down by Spencer.

"I'm going to blindfold you," he said now, which added an entirely new layer to the situation. For a moment she hesitated, but this was all about trust, and so she nodded as he tied one more scarf, this one a deep purple, over her eyes.

"Do you know why bondage is so powerful? It's more than just being about submission. It's about experiencing pleasure to the maximum."

"I don't know what you mean," she said.

"You will," he told her, and a few short minutes later, she realized he was right.

He'd started slowly, his fingertips tracing patterns on her skin. His mouth trailing kisses over her body. But then he stepped up the sensual torment. Teasing her erogenous zones. Sucking hard on her nipples, nibbling at her earlobe, licking the back of her knee. And, yes, teasing her clit mercilessly.

And with each stroke and each tease, the pleasure built and built until she twisted away, trying to escape it for just a little while, trying to bring a pleasure so intense that it bordered on pain back to a level that didn't have her body trembling and craving.

Trying, in other words, to gain back a modicum of control.

Bound, it was impossible. She didn't just experience pleasure, she endured it. And as that pleasure built and grew and rose and climbed, she couldn't deny that it was probably the most erotic experience of her life.

"Please," she begged, when she couldn't take it any more. When his teasing her in one spot and then moving to another had her body so on edge that it felt like every cell was on fire. "Please, Spencer, take me over."

"Are you sure?"

"Yes, oh, please yes."

He used his mouth and expert tongue to take her the

rest of the way, his hands holding her hips as she tried to squirm and twist under the unrelenting onslaught of pleasure. But it was no use, and she felt the power of a massive orgasm building inside of her, drawing her higher and higher until, finally, the intensity of sensations knocked her over the edge, sending her hurtling wildly into a maelstrom that rivaled the most violent of thunderstorms.

When, finally, she was breathing regularly again, Spencer untied her, then held her gently as she sighed with complete satisfaction. "Amazing," she said. "Wanna do it again?"

As she'd hoped, he laughed. "Yes, but let's wait for a night when it's not past three in the morning. Right now, I just want to hold you."

Since she was perfectly fine with that plan, she didn't protest. But she also wasn't sleepy, and her mind was spinning.

"Why didn't you do the final season of *Spencer's Place*?" she asked, snuggled up close to him. "Was it because of Brian?"

"Mostly," he said. "My money was still tied up with him. So I'd be working, and he'd be stealing. Seemed like a bad deal all around for me."

"I'd say."

He stroked a lazy pattern on her arm, and she sighed with bliss.

"On top of that," he continued, "the bloom had worn off. Back when I pitched it, I'd wanted the show for the work."

"I remember. You wanted to show people how to make repairs on their own place and flip a few properties at the same time. Don't stop that," she added, when he started to move his hand away.

He chuckled, but complied. "It was all Hollywood bull-shit. Or it felt like it. It just..." He trailed off with a shrug. "It wasn't fun."

She shifted out from under his touch, suddenly uncomfortable under the weight of a fresh guilt. "I'm sorry to pull you back into all that. I wouldn't have if—"

"No." He pressed a finger to her lips. "I didn't want to at first for a whole hell of a lot of reasons. But those reasons are gone. And now I'm having one of the best times of my life."

"Yeah?"

"Absolutely."

She snuggled close. "I'm glad."

"In fact, I was thinking that maybe we should try this again."

"This? You mean the show?"

"I've got another one waiting in the wings, remember? Would be a hell of a lot more fun fixing up the mansion with you."

"*Oh.*" For a second, Brooke wasn't sure she could breathe. She told herself he wasn't proposing marriage. All he wanted was to work with her installing drywall, laying tile, fixing plumbing, and the other eight million things the Drysdale Mansion needed. But that didn't change the fact that it was *their* place. That they'd be doing it together.

"Brooke? If you don't want to, it's okay."

"No," she blurted. "I do. But are you sure? We'll be on television. That whole celebrity thing, only this time we'll be under the microscope as a couple. Won't that drive you crazy?"

He squeezed her hand. "Why should it?" he asked. "After all, isn't that what we are?"

Chapter Eighteen

SPENCER LEARNED two things during Monday's Happy Hour. First, that Brooke looked sexy even when she was wearing reading glasses and pouring over the notes she'd made in her tiny, cramped handwriting. And second, that Parker Manning was a pig.

To be fair, Spencer didn't even know Parker's name when he made that assessment. But Spencer's radar had started ticking when the guy had entered the bar, noticed Brooke at a table with her laptop and notebook, and made a beeline straight for her.

Not surprising, of course. Parker was a man. And Brooke had that ethereal beauty coupled with the kind of easy curves that make a man take notice.

All well and good, except that Spencer didn't like it when a man other than himself did the noticing. And he especially didn't like it when Brooke leaped out of her chair and threw her arms around any guy who took it upon himself to look at her *that way*.

"Who is that?" he'd asked Mina. They'd been in the process of making a list of all the things that had to get finished before the bar opened its doors on Wednesday. An essential task, no doubt about that. But at the moment, it paled in the face of Spencer's need to know the identity of the pretty boy macking on his girlfriend.

Mina lifted herself up out of her seat and craned her neck. "Oh, that's Parker Manning," she said, and Spencer decided that not only was Parker a pig, but he had a prissy-ass name, too.

"Who the fuck is Parker Manning, and why is he hugging my girl?"

For a second, Mina looked like she was going to make some speech about how Brooke was her own woman and she was allowed to have male friends and on and on and on. But she probably caught sight of Spencer's face, because all she said was. "You know. Parker *Manning*. His dad's Bertram Manning."

Spencer shook his head, and Mina rolled her eyes. "Serious old Texas money family. Ranching. Oil. Tech. The whole nine yards. Parker could probably buy and sell this whole town just off the interest on his trust fund."

Yeah, definitely not liking the guy.

"As for the hug," Mina added, "you'll have to ask Brooke. But if I had to go out on a limb, I'd say they know each other."

"Then I guess it's time for me to make his acquaintance. Why don't you finish that list?"

"Okey-fine," she said, her lips trembling from withheld laughter.

"What?"

"You're such a guy, Spencer."

He considered that, shrugged, and said, "Thank you." Then he headed across the bar, fully intending to lay flat Parker Manning.

He didn't make it that far. Instead, he was stopped by a familiar female voice calling his name. He turned, and found Amy Rice standing behind him, her arms crossed over her chest, and her expression wary.

"Amy?" She'd been one of the production assistants on *Spencer's Place*, and as a general rule she didn't look so small and fragile. "What's the matter?"

"I keep trying to call you, but I couldn't. So I came here."

"Call me?" He pulled out his phone, but there were no missed calls.

"No, I meant that I tried, but I couldn't."

He frowned. The words were clear enough, but he wasn't catching the meaning. "Do you want to sit down? Maybe take this a little slower?"

She nodded, and he tried to swallow his worry. She'd been a freshman in college when she started working for the show, taking classes around the crazy production schedule. She'd been a hard worker and never shy about asking for projects or help or even a raise. So this hesitancy was completely out of character.

"It's okay, Amy. Whatever it is, I'll try to help."

The words worked like magic, and he watched as her shoulders sagged in relief. "Thank you. I really appreciate—well, just, thank you."

He waited, not wanting to rush her.

"So, the thing is—it's about Brian Shoal."

Spencer forced his expression to stay neutral. "Go on."

"Well, I know that you and he—well, he screwed you with the money stuff. I know that's all gossip, but—"

"It's true. What of it?"

"It's only—I mean—well, I thought if you knew something, then seeing as you probably don't much like him, you might be willing to tell me."

"Amy, you're going to have to back up and give me a little more information."

She sucked in a breath. "He raped me. He drugged me at a party and he raped me and I'm pressing charges. And my parents are helping me sue him civilly, too, and my attorney says if I can find someone else he did that to, then it will help my case a lot, and that's why I'm here. Can you help me?"

She blurted it out so fast he couldn't process all the words. But that was probably a good thing. Any more detail than what he picked up on, and he'd be too livid to think straight.

"Brian Shoal drugged and raped you?" He wanted to at least clarify that one, salient point.

She pressed her lips together, and she nodded. "I'm not lying. You might—"

"I believe you."

Her shoulders sagged with obvious relief. "Can you help me?"

He drew in a breath, temper warring with pity. "Whatever you need, you've got my full support."

"Then you know someone?"

Unfortunately, he thought he did.

Chapter Nineteen

"YOU'RE sure nothing's bothering you?" Brooke frowned at Spencer, who had his hands locked on the ten and two position of her sky blue Mini Cooper's steering wheel. "You can't possibly be jealous of Parker. I told you, he's an old friend from high school. And only a casual friend, too. We never even dated."

Spencer had always had a little bit of a jealous streak—she knew that. In the past, it had tended to show up when they met friends from her old neighborhood. As in, guys with significantly more money and definitely more pedigree. But back then she could usually get him to admit it and then laugh it off.

Today, not so much, and it worried her. Especially since Parker was a total non-issue. He'd noticed her, they'd talked, he'd left. End of story.

And yet here was Spencer, an hour later, still all bent out of shape.

Either he had some other bone to pick with Parker, or Parker wasn't really the issue at all.

Brooke's money was on the latter. But the problem was

that she didn't have a clue what was going on. And so far, Spencer wasn't talking. Instead, he seemed to be seething.

Frankly, enough was enough.

"Look, you know what? Drop me at home. You can keep the car for tonight. I'm not in the mood to deal with it or with you."

"I'm walking you in," he said, pulling into her driveway.

"Is that so? Are you leaving the attitude outside? Because if not, I think I can find my own damn door." Honestly, she wanted to cry. Which was stupid. This was just a dumb fight because Spencer got his hackles up about her talking to a gorgeous guy. Give it a day and it would fade away. It wasn't like they fought often, and in the grand scheme of things this was nothing.

Except it wasn't nothing. Because he wasn't talking.

And the silence was making her crazy.

He killed the engine, got out of the car, and headed to the front door. Which meant she either followed or slept in the car.

Fuck.

She followed, of course. And since he had a key to her place, he was already inside by the time she stepped into her foyer. "Enough," she called. "Tell me what's wrong or—"

"Tell me about this." He thrust a scarf at her. One that he'd used to bind her wrists just the other night.

She blinked up at him, confused.

"You said you trusted me." He waved the scarf in her face. "You had me tie your wrists so I'd know how deep your trust ran."

She felt her blood go cold. "Spencer," she said slowly. "What the hell is going on?"

He grabbed the scarf in the middle and actually ripped it in two. "Goddamn it, Brooke. You trust me with your most intimate emotions. With your fears. Your nightmares, but you don't trust me enough to tell me that the man who fucking raped you was a friend of mine? Of ours? That Brian fucked you a thousand times worse than he screwed me?"

Tears streamed down her face, but she didn't even realize she was crying until she tasted the salt in the corners of her mouth. "What— I mean, how—"

"He did the same thing to another girl. A woman who used to work for me. She came to me, told me because she was hoping I had evidence. She's pressing charges. I put the pieces together."

"I see." Since her knees were no longer working properly, she sank down onto the floor.

"You didn't trust me, Brooke." He held out the scarf. "This isn't trust. Not when you lie to me and tell me you don't know who did that to you. Not when it's a man we both once called a friend."

"No," she finally said, her voice steady. "I didn't tell you. Because I know you, Spencer. And if someone's fucking with your people, you're going to take action. And I couldn't lose you like that. You'd just told me that you wanted to put Brian in the ground after what he did to you. Do you think I don't know that you would do a thousand times worse for what he did to me?" A sob ripped out of her. "Do you think I wanted to see you arrested for assault? Or worse?"

"Like I said. You don't trust me."

"The hell I don't."

"No, you didn't trust me to protect you. You didn't trust me to handle myself. And you know what? Maybe you were right. After all, blood will tell, right? And my blood definitely isn't as blue as Parker's."

"Parker!"

"I'm just the guy with the brother in prison. A guy with a rap sheet for assault who lucked into a decent career because he's good with his goddamn hands. But don't ask him to do a real job, because he doesn't even know how to protect his own bank account much less the woman he loves."

"*Stop it.*" She slammed her hand back against the wall, making it reverberate through the small entrance hall. "Do not put this on me. *You* see yourself that way, Spencer Dean. And you know what? That's your problem. I get that you're upset—I am, too. But don't you dare take it out on me."

She didn't bother to wipe away the tears that rolled down her cheeks. He was such a stubborn, goddamn ass.

He made a fist, then pounded it against her wall once, and then once again. He stood, breathing hard. When he spoke, his voice was level. "I heard what your father said. The day he came to offer to finance your company. He said that sooner or later I'd disappoint you. Well, I guess maybe today is sooner."

"Yeah," she said, her body limp with exhaustion and way too tired to fight anymore. "Yeah, I guess maybe it is."

He took a step toward her, then paused.

Her heart hitched, and she wanted to reach for him. To tell him that he was her everything. That he didn't know his own worth. That him holding her and making love to her was a thousand times more powerful than his fist in Brian's face.

But the problem was that she could tell him that every day for the rest of their lives, and until he truly believed that she loved him the way he was, they'd never be clear. And she couldn't live waiting for the other shoe to drop.

Slowly, she stood up, then walked toward her living room. She paused long enough to look back over her shoulder. "I'll see you at work tomorrow," she said, forcing herself not to cry. "You know the way out."

Chapter Twenty

"IS IT JUST SPENCER, or are all men thick-skulled idiots?"

"I think it's all men," Amanda said. She glanced sideways at Jenna. "You got an opinion?"

"Definitely all. Although I have Reece trained pretty well."

"That's right," Amanda said. "She does. So, see? Men are trainable. That's good, right? All you have to do is get Spencer one of those little collars with the electric shock, and then when he goes out of bounds, zap him."

Brooke laughed out loud, which was a good feeling considering she'd cried herself empty last night. She'd come to work as usual, but Spencer was off getting lumber, and so she locked herself up in the office and put in an SOS call to Amanda. Jenna hadn't started out as part of the conversation, but had poked her head in to deliver a message and gotten waylaid by Amanda. Which was pretty much what happened to most people around Amanda.

"Thanks, you guys. I have no idea what I'm going to do, but I feel better."

"I don't even know the real issue here," Jenna said.

"But in my experience if a guy goes off the rails, he usually gets himself back on track. I mean, the bottom line here is that he loves you. Anyone who's been hanging around The Fix for the last two weeks can see that."

"Is that enough?"

"If it's not, we'll take him out back and throw rotten food at him until he sees reason. Deal?"

Brooke sighed, then blinked back another round of tears. "I love you guys. And I really hope it doesn't come to rotten food."

"It won't. Spencer's a good guy."

True enough. The problem was that Spencer didn't know how good he was. But Brooke had taken enough of Jenna's time, and that wasn't a problem the girls could help with anyway. "Did you say you had a message?"

"Oh, damn. I forgot. I swear, my head is so cloudy these days."

Brooke almost said she wasn't surprised, then remembered that Jenna hadn't actually told anyone she was pregnant, so she kept her mouth shut.

"There's a man to see you," Jenna said to Brooke. "He says he's your father."

Brooke met Amanda's eyes, who looked back at her with all the sympathy of a true friend. She didn't, however, offer to meet the beast in Brooke's place.

"I could tell him you have a slight case of Ebola," Amanda suggested. "That he can see you, but he needs a hazmat suit?"

"It's a thought," Brooke said. "But probably best I get it over with."

She walked neither slowly nor quickly, not wanting to face him, but also not wanting to prolong the pain. And when she finally reached his table, he was impatiently tapping the dial of his Rolex.

"There you are."

"I was in the middle of something," she said. "If you expected to see me at a specific time, an appointment would have been handy."

"I understand you're still doing this ridiculous show."

"Yup." She forced herself to say nothing else. He was the one who'd taught her that—if you're on the witness stand, the fewer words, the better.

"Mmmm. Your mother and I are disappointed."

"Color me shocked."

"For God's sake, Brooke, don't be impertinent. I'm only making conversation."

She sighed. "Daddy, you and I both know that conversation is that last reason you're here. Tell me what the first is and let's get on with it."

"To be blunt, I've had enough. You had your fun with that boy years ago, and now it's time for you to move on. Do this job if you must, but that is not the kind of person we need in this family."

"Oh, really? Because I'm thinking someone with a real sense of family, who loves unconditionally and who's worked his ass off to get where he is actually qualifies as *exactly* the kind of person we should want in this family."

Assuming, of course, that she and Spencer were still a couple. But surely they were. They couldn't really be over, could they? Surely Spencer didn't really see himself the way her father saw him.

"He is a criminal."

"The hell he is." Out of the corner of her eye, she saw Cameron wiping down a nearby table, and she lowered her voice. "He has a record from when he was a kid and his world was falling apart. I'd like to see you survive what he lived through. Because, Daddy, I don't think you could have made it."

Her father drew in a breath and sat straighter in his chair. "Do not speak to me like that."

"Then don't come here asking for it." She drew her own breath and started to push her chair back. "Are we done?"

"We are not."

Resigned, she settled back into her chair. "Go ahead."

"Perhaps you recall that I have ties to the parole board."

Fingers of dread latched onto her spine. "Yes?"

"It seems that Richard Dean's case is being evaluated right now. One call, and I can ensure that he stays in prison. Not just today, but until he rots in that cell."

The dread morphed into cold terror.

"You can't possibly be that cruel."

"Cruel to keep a convicted murderer in prison? I think you have confused your adjectives."

She swallowed.

"There's a simple solution. You want Richard Dean paroled? Then walk away from Spencer. That's it. Easy as pie. You did it once before, after all. And you built yourself a successful business. Don't let him drag you down."

Her heart was pounding so hard in her chest that she thought it might explode. But she could do this. She *had* to.

She took a breath, then faced her father. "You know what, Daddy. *Do it.*"

His eyes went wide. "Very well." He started to rise.

"But know that if you do, I'll fuck you up so good you'll never be elected to the bench again. Hell, you'll be lucky not to be disbarred. Every line you've pulled, every threat you've made, I'll make sure it's out there. And in case you haven't noticed, I have access to television and social media now. I have a platform, Daddy. Don't give me a grudge to go with it."

She stood, then aimed her best smile at him. The one he and her mother had paid for, actually. "I'm going back to work now, but feel free to order a drink before you go. I recommend the Jalapeño Margaritas. They have one hell of a kick."

Chapter Twenty-One

SPENCER HAD SEEN Brooke only in glimpses on Tuesday, and he was smart enough to know that was intentional. But whether it was because she was giving him space or had washed her hands of him, he wasn't entirely sure.

He hoped it was the first. He'd been an asshole Monday night—he knew that. Hell, he probably would have picked up on that little detail even if Brooke hadn't done such a damn good—and thorough—job of calling him out.

He had no excuse, only explanations. He'd been burning up with jealousy, as potent as any fever he'd ever experienced. Foolish, probably. Hell, Spencer didn't know Parker Manning from Adam, but the guy had definitely gotten under his skin. Because Parker had class and breeding and money. Not to mention the kind of clean-cut good looks that landed on billboards and magazine pages.

What Spencer had forgotten was what Parker *didn't* have; Parker didn't have Brooke. Spencer did.

And that's where his second explanation-not-excuse

came into play. *Fear*. Because Spencer had looked at Parker and had felt a cold wave of debilitating fear rise up with the knowledge that while Brooke might be his right then, there was no guarantee that he could keep her. Hell, he'd lost her before. And God knew there were a hell of a lot better men in the world for her than him. So why the fuck should he be the lucky one?

She swore he was. Maybe she even believed it.

But he was having hell of a hard time believing it himself.

"Hey, you guys!" Mina's cheery voice cut through the din in the back bar that was being used as a staging area for the guys. Behind her, he could hear the muffled chatter of the emcee, an indie film star that Jenna considered an absolute coup for the contest.

"So the way it works is that you'll walk down the red carpet, climb the stairs, and then you can say a one-liner if you want. Like *A vote for me is a vote for hotness* or whatever. And you really ought to take your shirt off," she added, grinning as she pointed a finger toward a still-reluctant Cameron.

"Then you strut your stuff back here until everyone's gone. Then you'll all come back, line up on the stage, and the audience will cast their votes. Then you all get to mingle once the ballots are collected until we announce a half hour or so later."

She turned her attention to Spencer. "Since you're last, you don't have to come back. Stay on the stage, and these guys will join you."

"You got it."

In the main bar, the music started, and the first of the twelve started that direction. Some of the others gathered in the doorway to watch, but Spencer didn't bother. He wasn't nervous; he'd had too many years in the spotlight for nerves to catch up to him now. But he wished he was. Nerves would give him something to think about other than Brooke.

As much for the distraction as for friendship, he eased over toward Cameron. "They finally talked you into it, huh?"

Cameron shrugged. "I figured I'd never live it down if I didn't do it. But I'm doing it my way."

Spencer nodded slowly, not sure what the kid meant. "Your way? I'm guessing you're not taking your shirt off."

A sly grin touched Cam's face. "Wait and see."

That, at least, gave Spencer something to ponder for the rest of the wait.

Cam was number eleven, and as the kid headed up the red carpet, Spence moved to the doorway so he could watch—and the first thing he saw was Brooke, a few yards away and moving straight toward him.

"Hey," she said, when she reached the staging area's doorway.

"Hey, back."

A smile flickered on her lips, and she reached into the room, her hand extended for his. He took it, awareness coursing through him. This was Brooke. And, dammit, she was his.

"I wanted to wish you luck," she said. "And if you fall off our amazing new stage, I'll have to kill you."

He laughed, a little bit more than the joke deserved, but it felt so damn good to be civilized.

"Listen," he said, but he never got any further, because the entire room had burst into laughter and applause.

Brooke and Spencer both looked toward the stage, shifting this way and that to better see the spectacle of

Cameron Reed, bartender extraordinaire, standing shirt-less on the stage, the words *Comic Relief* written across his chest in what looked like lipstick, and a big arrow pointing up toward his head.

"Oh my," Brooke said. "At least he didn't *really* go for self-deprecating and aim that arrow the other direction."

Spencer snorted with laughter, and Brooke stepped into the staging area long enough to press a gentle kiss to his temple. "Knock 'em dead," she whispered, then faded back into the crowd right as his music began.

He made the trek to the stage, then sauntered across, making it a point to smile at all the women who were laughing and shouting for him to take off the shirt. Of course, he complied, then did a Mr. Universe-style pose, showing off front and back, before nodding to the crowd and then stepping to the rear of the stage as the other guys joined him for the line-up.

After that, he and the rest mingled in the crowd, where he and Cam were definitely drawing the most attention. He tried to find Brooke in the crush, but never managed to lay eyes on her.

He didn't see her again, in fact, until the emcee, Beverly, called for attention, and all the men trooped duti-fully back onto the stage to get the results.

"A drumroll, please," Beverly said, and synthesized drums poured from the speakers. "And, ladies and gentlemen—but mostly ladies—your vote for Mr. February is *Spencer Dean*."

The place burst into applause and Spencer went forward to get the Mr. February T-shirt that Beverly was holding out for him as a prize. Molly and Andy were going to love this, *that* he knew for certain.

He was about to pull on the tee when he finally caught

sight of Brooke in the audience. He'd expected her to be watching him, but instead, she was turned sideways, looking at someone in the audience, her eyes wide as if with fear and her skin as pale as death. *What the hell?*

He shifted, and when he followed her gaze, his entire body turned hot, burning with a heated rage that even brimstone couldn't match.

Brian.

Standing right there, his eyes on Brooke. His feet moving toward her.

No way. No fucking way.

He didn't think. He just acted. And the next thing he knew he'd leaped off the stage, grabbed the bastard's collar, and landed a brutal punch right on Brian's traitorous, fucked up, aristocratic nose.

He felt it crack beneath his hand. Smelled the unmistakable tang of blood. Heard Brian's howl as he went down, clutching his face as blood seeped through his fingers. Saw chairs scrape backwards and customers leap to their feet.

None of it made any sense. The wildness was still alive within him, and he shifted his stance, ready to pounce on Brian and fucking *end* him.

Brooke's hand on his arm stopped him, and he looked up to see her tear-streaked face.

Immediately, everything drained out of him, and he had to reach out and grab a nearby table to keep his legs from collapsing under him.

"Spenc—"

He didn't let her finish. "I'm sorry," he said, then turned and stumbled toward the door.

THE PANIC that had filled Brooke upon seeing Brian still coursed through her veins, only now it had a different character. Now, she was afraid for Spencer.

"Spencer!" she called as he pushed his way through the crowd. She tried to follow, but a strong hand on her arm stopped her. She tried to jerk free, turned, and saw that it was Easton.

"Let him go," he said gently.

"But—"

Brent had pushed his way through the crowd and joined them. "Mina's called an ambulance. Is that guy okay? And what the hell was that all about?"

It was the voice of a cop, direct and to the point, but not without sympathy.

"I need to go find Spencer," Brooke said, realizing that she was crying. And that Casper and Nick were both hovering nearby. She wiped her nose on the back of her hand. Right then, being on camera was the least of her problems.

The world around her had fallen into slow motion. Tyree and Jenna and Reece had arrived to help Brian, and Brooke didn't have the energy to tell them he didn't deserve help. Easton and Brent were focused on her.

"Let's go to the back," Easton said. Brent nodded, and they led her to Tyree's office.

"Do you know what happened in there?" Brent asked. "More importantly, *why* it happened?"

Slowly, she nodded. And for only the second time in her life, she told the story of what happened with her and Brian, starting with their history as friends, then up to the day Brian raped her.

"Spencer knows," she said. "I told him a few days ago. Or, actually, I guess I should say I told him that I'd been

173

date raped. He figured out the Brian part. There's a woman—Amy. She's a former employee of his, and she's pressing charges against Brian. She came to Spencer to see if he knew about any other victims, and he realized what Brian did to me."

The two men looked at each other, but said nothing.

"He had other reasons, too," she said, then told them about the financial shenanigans that Brian had been into.

Slowly, Easton nodded.

"I need to go find him," Brooke said. "Can I go now? Please?"

Brent laid a hand on her arm. "The man's a live wire right now, sweetheart. Give him until tomorrow morning."

"But—" She drew a breath, powering through the fear. "But what if they find him and arrest him?"

"My first job was with the District Attorney's office," Easton said. "Let me make a few calls. And I also want to poke into this Amy thing. Even if the case isn't pending in Travis County, I might be able to learn something. I'll even go down to the police department and start there."

"I'll go with you," Brent said. "Odds are good I'll know somebody who can help us out. It's going to be okay," he added, giving her a quick hug. "Don't worry."

But that was easier said than done.

Chapter Twenty-Two

SPENCER HEARD the rusty hinges of the mansion's kitchen door creak, and he stood to meet her. He knew it would be Brooke, and he knew why she'd stayed away last night. Because he'd fucked up. Proven himself to be the man she'd always feared him to be. A man whose life was in his hands, not his head.

"So there you go," he said, as she stepped into the room, her face pale and drawn. "That's me. That's the kind of man I am. And I know you can't handle—"

"Shut up, Spencer."

He did, mostly because her words shocked him into silence.

She moved slowly toward him, then took his hands. And as his heart flipped over, she gently bent and kissed his bruised knuckles. "For a guy who's made so much of himself, you can be pretty damn stupid. You know that, right?"

"Made—"

"You think you're not a success because you work with your hands and don't know how to do double-digit accounting? That's bullshit. You're capable and honest and loyal and you would lay down your life for someone you loved." She blinked, and a tear spilled down her cheek.

He held his breath, not sure what she was saying to him. Wanting to believe, but scared to take the leap.

He drew a breath, then decided to cut to the chase. "You didn't tell me about Brian because you were afraid I'd do what I did last night."

"Exactly."

"Well, I'm sorry, but this is who I am. And if—"

"Christ, do I have to hit you over the head with a brick? How many times do I have to tell you before it penetrates your thick skull? I don't give a fuck that you beat the shit out of that ass wipe. Do you think I don't understand how much it hurt you to hear what he did to me? To know that there was nothing you could do to erase that? Don't you know that I would have happily smashed his face in all by myself?"

"But—"

"But *nothing*." She drew in a breath, apparently gathering control. Or possibly considering kicking him in the shins.

"Come on, Spencer. I wanted to stand up and cheer when you punched him. I don't think less of you for protecting me—if anything, you get mega-brownie points in my book. But I swear to God, if you screwed things up for us by getting nailed with an assault charge—"

"Us?" The word had lassoed his heart, and he was having a hard time breathing.

She squared her shoulders and looked so put out with him that it was all he could do not to pull her close and kiss the expression right off her face.

"We had a fight," she said. "We'll probably have more.

176

Do you really think that was the end of us? Because screw that. I'm not letting go that easily, Spencer Dean. Even if you do have the thickest skull on the planet."

She moved in front of him, then poked him in the chest with her forefinger. Hard. "You. This man. This guy right in front of me. He's who I want. Who I've always wanted. And you're not getting away from me without a fight."

"Angel," he said, barely able to get the endearment past his clogged throat. He reached for her, and then she was in his arms, and he knew that no man in the world had ever been luckier. "I love you," he said.

"I love you, too," she said, her tone a little exasperated. Then she shifted in his embrace so she could see his face. "Oh, and by the way. We're trending on social media."

He laughed. A full-on, hearty laugh. And damned but it felt good.

At least until he remembered.

"I left a crime scene," he said. "I need to go turn myself in." He raked his fingers through his hair.

"That's what I mean," she said. "You're an honorable man." She pulled out of his embrace and took her phone out of her pocket. "I'll go with you. But let me talk to Easton or Brent first."

"Why—" he began, but then his own phone rang. He pulled it out, his chest tightening when he saw the number. And as Brooke moved away to have her own conversation, he answered the call from Richie's attorney.

When he hung up, he felt numb. As if his limbs had entirely disappeared. He sank to the ground and stared at his phone. Just stared at it until Brooke knelt in front of him, asking him what the hell was wrong.

"It's Richie," he said, then felt his face break into a smile as reality settled over him. "He's been paroled."

Her hand went to her mouth, and tears streamed down her eyes as she threw her arms around him and hugged him. He held her tight, not wanting to let go. Not ever wanting to let go. But after what seemed like an eternity, she squirmed free, then sat on her heels, grinning at him.

"Let me add a cherry on top this already awesome day. You're clear."

He blinked, confused. "Come again?"

"Brent and Easton have been working with the cops and the DA and Amy's attorney all last night and this morning. I'm going to swear an affidavit, and Brian's going to plead guilty to two counts of aggravated assault. And you, my hero, get to walk."

"So that's it? I don't have to go down to the station?"

"Easton says that Amy might ask you—and me—to be a witness in their civil case. But they think Brian will settle that anyway. So no. Nothing you have to do now." She grinned. "I'd say it's turning out to be a pretty good day."

"The best," he said, pulling her against him and pressing a kiss to the top of her head. "You know, once I wanted this house because it would be proof that I was worth more than where I came from."

"And now?"

"Now I want it because it's where I'm most at peace with you."

He felt her tremble in his arms. Then she tilted her face back, looking at him with eyes so full of love they humbled him. "Spencer," she said, "make love to me."

It was a demand he wasn't about to refuse, and he pulled her close, then kissed her gently, letting their passion build as they helped each other out of their clothes, spreading them out of the floor to make a pad in the middle of the house that would soon be their home.

"Now," she said, tugging him down so that he was balanced on top of her, looking deep into eyes so full of love it filled his soul.

He took her tenderly, claiming her body under a battered roof with the wide blue sky above them, a shaft of sunlight cutting through the dust and making her skin glow.

And when she arched up, crying his name so that it echoed against those crumbling walls, Spencer knew that no man had ever been luckier.

Later, as he drifted off with Brooke in his arms and the old Drysdale place rising up around them, Spencer felt something shift inside him. A need settling. A monster sleeping.

He'd done it, finally. Spencer Dean was home and safe, wrapped in the embrace of the woman he loved. A woman who loved him right back.

Epilogue

The Night of the Mr. February Competition

CAMERON REED SLID a Loaded Corona down the bar to Matthew Herrington, one of the regulars who owned a nearby gym where Cameron worked out. His attention wasn't on Matthew, however. It was on Mina.

He could barely see her from this angle. Just a few flashes of her midnight black hair, so sleek it seemed to reflect a blue hue under the vibrant stage lights. It was almost two, and the place had mostly cleared out, calm enough now that he could hear Mina laughing with Jenna, talking about how if they'd wanted drama in their first episode, they couldn't have planned it any better.

Cam had no idea what the whole thing had been about. All he knew was that Spencer had tossed aside the Mr. February T-shirt then leaped off the stage and landed a solid punch in some Robert Redford look-alike's face.

Everyone in The Fix had been shocked, but from the guy's expression, he'd probably had it coming.

Other than that, the only thing Cam knew was that

Spencer had done it for a woman. That much he could tell from the look of adoration mixed with the shock in Brooke's eyes.

Cam sighed, wanting to see that expression on Mina. More accurately, wanting to see it when she looked at him. And only at him.

Tonight, he'd gotten the reaction he'd intended from her and the whole bar, but raucous laughter wasn't what he craved.

"You've got it bad, buddy," Matthew said, and Cam turned sharply to look at the gym owner.

"What? No. I'm just zoning out. Staring into space."

"Tell me another one."

Cam scowled.

"Better yet, tell it to the girl." Matthew lifted his bottle in a salute, then took a long swallow.

"That what you'd do?"

"Hell to the yes," Matthew said.

"How?"

Matthew leaned back. He had an angular face and eyes full of humor. Right now, those eyes were dancing with mirth. "Damned if I know, kid. But if you want her, you need to figure it out." He took another swallow. "*Do* you want her?"

Cameron looked out over the crowd, his eyes immediately finding Mina. "Hell to the yes," he whispered.

Now he just had to figure out how to get her.

The Men of Man of the Month!

Are you eager to learn which Man of the Month book features which sexy hero?

Here's a handy list!

Down On Me - meet Reece
Hold On Tight - meet Spencer
Need You Now - meet Cameron
Start Me Up - meet Nolan
Get It On - meet Tyree
In Your Eyes - meet Parker
Turn Me On - meet Derek
Shake It Up - meet Landon
All Night Long - meet Easton
In Too Deep - meet Matthew
Light My Fire - meet Griffin
Walk The Line - meet Brent

and don't miss Bar Bites: A Man of the Month Cookbook that includes a short story featuring Eric, slices of life, and bonus scenes for all the men!

Need You Now Sneak Peek

Please enjoy this fun, unedited peek at Need You Now!

Cameron Reed sat on the edge of the bed, every nerve in his body crackling with heat and anticipation.

It was finally happening. *Mina.* Thank God, she was finally his.

He shifted, and the springs in the cheap motel mattress squeaked, making him jump. He bit his lip, hating that he was so on edge. But this moment—this whole night—was momentous. The best night of his life. Hell, the best night in history as far as he was concerned, and Cam had read one hell of a lot of history books.

He'd been in love with Mina Silver for half his life, and he'd known her longer than that. She was his best friend's twin sister, after all, so she'd been a constant presence. The girl they teased, the pest they shooed away.

Or she had been, until Cam had begun to notice her sweet smile, her quirky sense of humor. Until he realized that half the time when he went to Darryl's house after school, his motive was less about playing video games with his buddy and more about catching a glimpse of Mina.

And then one day, he'd caught a glimpse of her making out with Tony Renfroe, the most popular guy in middle school.

That's when the monster had stirred inside Cameron. A wild, craving beast that had wanted to lash out and knock Tony right off his pedestal—and out of Mina's arms.

Except he hadn't given in to that monster. Not then. Not later.

And Mina had dated Tony. Then Alex. Then Roger. And God only knew who else.

But she'd never dated him. Never even thought about him like that. They were friends—hell, they were practically family.

Until now.

He had no idea how he'd gotten so lucky to have finally caught her attention, but he had, and she was here with him now. In this motel. And sex was most definitely on the agenda.

He swallowed, nerves tingling as he waited. She'd disappeared into the tiny bathroom to get ready, and had brushed her finger over his lips with a promise to be right back.

Christ, the waiting was killing him. He was hyperaware of everything. The buzz of the air conditioner. The scratch of the rough bedspread. The sound of the water running in the bathroom.

And then—*oh, God*—the subtle click of the doorknob turning and the creak of hinges as the bathroom door opened.

She stepped out, clad in a short terrycloth robe that

ended at the top of her thighs and revealed miles of perfect legs. She walked toward him, and he swallowed, knowing without seeing that she was naked underneath. That all she had to do was loosen the tie at her waist and open the robe to reveal herself to him. Her firm breasts, her flat belly, her entire body that he intended to drop down onto his knees to worship.

"Are you ready for me?" she whispered, and he felt his cock go hard.

He nodded, his mouth too dry to speak. And when she took another step toward him and pulled loose the sash, he thought his heart might stop.

But that was nothing compared to when her hands went to the robe, and she started to pull it open. To reveal herself to him. To stand naked before him and—

Bang!

A wave of golden light burst from the robe, blinding him and knocking him backward.

And when he'd blinked enough to clear his vision, she was gone.

Just gone.

What the hell?

He tried to catch his breath and clear his muddled head. Slowly, he looked around his room, then gasped at what he was seeing.

His room. Not a rundown motel. Not a bed with squeaky springs. And most definitely not a room that Mina shared.

It had all been a dream.

A wonderful, delicious, incredible dream—and he'd awakened to a nightmare. Because he didn't really have Mina—he never had.

But, goddammit, he would.

Enough waiting. Enough dreaming.

It was time for Cameron to get the girl he craved, or die trying.

Who's Your Man of the Month?

When a group of fiercely determined friends realize their beloved hang-out is in danger of closing, they take matters into their own hands to bring back customers lost to a competing bar. Fighting fire with a heat of their own, they double down with the broad shoulders, six-pack abs, and bare chests of dozens of hot, local guys who they cajole, prod, and coerce into auditioning for a Man of the Month calendar.

But it's not just the fate of the bar that's at stake. Because as things heat up, each of the men meets his match in this sexy, flirty, and compelling binge-read romance series of twelve novels releasing every other week from *New York Times* bestselling author J. Kenner.

"With each novel featuring a favorite romance trope— beauty and the beast, billionaire bad boys, friends to lovers, second chance romance, secret baby, and more—[the Man of the Month] series hits the heart and soul of romance." *New York Times* bestselling author Carly Phillips

Down On Me
Hold On Tight
Need You Now

Start Me Up
Get It On
In Your Eyes
Turn Me On
Shake It Up
All Night Long
In Too Deep
Light My Fire
Walk The Line

and don't miss Bar Bites: A Man of the Month Cookbook!

Down On Me excerpt

Did you miss book one in the Man of the Month series? Here's an excerpt from Down On Me!

Chapter One

Reece Walker ran his palms over the slick, soapy ass of the woman in his arms and knew that he was going straight to hell.

Not because he'd slept with a woman he barely knew. Not because he'd enticed her into bed with a series of well-timed bourbons and particularly inventive half-truths. Not even because he'd lied to his best friend Brent about why Reece couldn't drive with him to the airport to pick up Jenna, the third player in their trifecta of lifelong friendship.

No, Reece was staring at the fiery pit because he was a lame, horny asshole without the balls to tell the naked beauty standing in the shower with him that she wasn't the woman he'd been thinking about for the last four hours.

And if that wasn't one of the pathways to hell, it damn sure ought to be.

He let out a sigh of frustration, and Megan tilted her head, one eyebrow rising in question as she slid her hand down to stroke his cock, which was demonstrating no guilt whatsoever about the whole going to hell issue. "Am I boring you?"

"Hardly." That, at least, was the truth. He felt like a prick, yes. But he was a well-satisfied one. "I was just thinking that you're beautiful."

She smiled, looking both shy and pleased—and Reece felt even more like a heel. What the devil was wrong with him? She *was* beautiful. And hot and funny and easy to talk to. Not to mention good in bed.

But she wasn't Jenna, which was a ridiculous comparison. Because Megan qualified as fair game, whereas Jenna was one of his two best friends. She trusted him. Loved him. And despite the way his cock perked up at the thought of doing all sorts of delicious things with her in bed, Reece knew damn well that would never happen. No way was he risking their friendship. Besides, Jenna didn't love him like that. Never had, never would.

And that—plus about a billion more reasons—meant that Jenna was entirely off-limits.

Too bad his vivid imagination hadn't yet gotten the memo.

Fuck it.

He tightened his grip, squeezing Megan's perfect rear. "Forget the shower," he murmured. "I'm taking you back to bed." He needed this. Wild. Hot. Demanding. And dirty enough to keep him from thinking.

Hell, he'd scorch the earth if that's what it took to burn Jenna from his mind—and he'd leave Megan limp, whimpering, and very, very satisfied. His guilt. Her pleasure. At least it would be a win for one of them.

And who knows? Maybe he'd manage to fuck the fantasies of his best friend right out of his head.

It didn't work.

Reece sprawled on his back, eyes closed, as Megan's gentle fingers traced the intricate outline of the tattoos inked across his pecs and down his arms. Her touch was warm and tender, in stark contrast to the way he'd just fucked her—a little too wild, a little too hard, as if he were fighting a battle, not making love.

Well, that was true, wasn't it?

But it was a battle he'd lost. Victory would have brought oblivion. Yet here he was, a naked woman beside him, and his thoughts still on Jenna, as wild and intense and impossible as they'd been since that night eight months ago when the earth had shifted beneath him, and he'd let himself look at her as a woman and not as a friend.

One breathtaking, transformative night, and Jenna didn't even realize it. And he'd be damned if he'd ever let her figure it out.

Beside him, Megan continued her exploration, one fingertip tracing the outline of a star. "No names? No wife or girlfriend's initials hidden in the design?"

He turned his head sharply, and she burst out laughing.

"Oh, don't look at me like that." She pulled the sheet up to cover her breasts as she rose to her knees beside him. "I'm just making conversation. No hidden agenda at all. Believe me, the last thing I'm interested in is a relationship." She scooted away, then sat on the edge of the bed, giving him an enticing view of her bare back. "I don't even do overnights."

As if to prove her point, she bent over, grabbed her bra off the floor, and started getting dressed.

"Then that's one more thing we have in common." He pushed himself up, rested his back against the headboard, and enjoyed the view as she wiggled into her jeans.

"Good," she said, with such force that he knew she meant it, and for a moment he wondered what had soured her on relationships.

As for himself, he hadn't soured so much as fizzled. He'd had a few serious girlfriends over the years, but it never worked out. No matter how good it started, invariably the relationship crumbled. Eventually, he had to acknowledge that he simply wasn't relationship material. But that didn't mean he was a monk, the last eight months notwithstanding.

She put on her blouse and glanced around, then slipped her feet into her shoes. Taking the hint, he got up and pulled on his jeans and T-shirt. "Yes?" he asked, noticing the way she was eying him speculatively.

"The truth is, I was starting to think you might be in a relationship."

"What? Why?"

She shrugged. "You were so quiet there for a while, I wondered if maybe I'd misjudged you. I thought you might be married and feeling guilty."

Guilty.

The word rattled around in his head, and he groaned. "Yeah, you could say that."

"Oh, *hell*. Seriously?"

"No," he said hurriedly. "Not that. I'm not cheating on my non-existent wife. I wouldn't. Not ever." Not in small part because Reece wouldn't ever have a wife since he thought the institution of marriage was a crock, but he didn't see the need to explain that to Megan.

"But as for guilt?" he continued. "Yeah, tonight I've got that in spades."

She relaxed slightly. "Hmm. Well, sorry about the guilt, but I'm glad about the rest. I have rules, and I consider myself a good judge of character. It makes me cranky when I'm wrong."

"Wouldn't want to make you cranky."

"Oh, you really wouldn't. I can be a total bitch." She sat on the edge of the bed and watched as he tugged on his boots. "But if you're not hiding a wife in your attic, what are you feeling guilty about? I assure you, if it has anything to do with my satisfaction, you needn't feel guilty at all." She flashed a mischievous grin, and he couldn't help but smile back. He hadn't invited a woman into his bed for eight long months. At least he'd had the good fortune to pick one he actually liked.

"It's just that I'm a crappy friend," he admitted.

"I doubt that's true."

"Oh, it is," he assured her as he tucked his wallet into his back pocket. The irony, of course, was that as far as Jenna knew, he was an excellent friend. The best. One of her two pseudo-brothers with whom she'd sworn a blood oath the summer after sixth grade, almost twenty years ago.

From Jenna's perspective, Reece was at least as good as Brent, even if the latter scored bonus points because he was picking Jenna up at the airport while Reece was trying to fuck his personal demons into oblivion. Trying anything, in fact, that would exorcise the memory of how she'd clung to him that night, her curves enticing and her breath intoxicating, and not just because of the scent of too much alcohol.

She'd trusted him to be the white knight, her noble rescuer, and all he'd been able to think about was the feel of her body, soft and warm against his, as he carried her up the stairs to her apartment.

A wild craving had hit him that night, like a tidal wave of emotion crashing over him, washing away the outer shell of friendship and leaving nothing but raw desire and a longing so potent it nearly brought him to his knees.

It had taken all his strength to keep his distance when the only thing he'd wanted was to cover every inch of her naked body with kisses. To stroke her skin and watch her writhe with pleasure.

He'd won a hard-fought battle when he reined in his desire that night. But his victory wasn't without its wounds. She'd pierced his heart when she'd drifted to sleep in his arms, whispering that she loved him—and he knew that she meant it only as a friend.

More than that, he knew that he was the biggest asshole to ever walk the earth.

Thankfully, Jenna remembered nothing of that night. The liquor had stolen her memories, leaving her with a monster hangover, and him with a Jenna-shaped hole in his heart.

"Well?" Megan pressed. "Are you going to tell me? Or do I have to guess?"

"I blew off a friend."

"Yeah? That probably won't score you points in the Friend of the Year competition, but it doesn't sound too dire. Unless you were the best man and blew off the wedding? Left someone stranded at the side of the road somewhere in West Texas? Or promised to feed their cat and totally forgot? Oh, God. Please tell me you didn't kill Fluffy."

He bit back a laugh, feeling slightly better. "A friend came in tonight, and I feel like a complete shit for not meeting her plane."

"Well, there are taxis. And I assume she's an adult?"

"She is, and another friend is there to pick her up."

"I see," she said, and the way she slowly nodded suggested that she saw too much. "I'm guessing that *friend* means *girlfriend*? Or, no. You wouldn't do that. So she must be an ex."

"Really not," he assured her. "Just a friend. Lifelong, since sixth grade."

"Oh, I get it. Longtime friend. High expectations. She's going to be pissed."

"Nah. She's cool. Besides, she knows I usually work nights."

"Then what's the problem?"

He ran his hand over his shaved head, the bristles from the day's growth like sandpaper against his palm. "Hell if I know," he lied, then forced a smile, because whether his problem was guilt or lust or just plain stupidity, she hardly deserved to be on the receiving end of his bullshit.

He rattled his car keys. "How about I buy you one last drink before I take you home?"

"You're sure you don't mind a working drink?" Reece asked as he helped Megan out of his cherished baby blue vintage Chevy pickup. "Normally I wouldn't take you to my job, but we just hired a new bar back, and I want to see how it's going."

He'd snagged one of the coveted parking spots on Sixth Street, about a block down from The Fix, and he glanced automatically toward the bar, the glow from the windows relaxing him. He didn't own the place, but it was like a second home to him and had been for one hell of a long time.

"There's a new guy in training, and you're not there? I thought you told me you were the manager?"

"I did, and I am, but Tyree's there. The owner, I mean. He's always on site when someone new is starting. Says it's his job, not mine. Besides, Sunday's my day off, and Tyree's a stickler for keeping to the schedule."

"Okay, but why are you going then?"

"Honestly? The new guy's my cousin. He'll probably give me shit for checking in on him, but old habits die hard." Michael had been almost four when Vincent died, and the loss of his dad hit him hard. At sixteen, Reece had tried to be stoic, but Uncle Vincent had been like a second father to him, and he'd always thought of Mike as more brother than cousin. Either way, from that day on, he'd made it his job to watch out for the kid.

"Nah, he'll appreciate it," Megan said. "I've got a little sister, and she gripes when I check up on her, but it's all for show. She likes knowing I have her back. And as for getting a drink where you work, I don't mind at all."

As a general rule, late nights on Sunday were dead, both in the bar and on Sixth Street, the popular downtown Austin street that had been a focal point of the city's nightlife for decades. Tonight was no exception. At half-past one in the morning, the street was mostly deserted. Just a few cars moving slowly, their headlights shining toward the west, and a smattering of couples, stumbling and laughing. Probably tourists on their way back to one of the downtown hotels.

It was late April, though, and the spring weather was drawing both locals and tourists. Soon, the area—and the bar—would be bursting at the seams. Even on a slow Sunday night.

Situated just a few blocks down from Congress Avenue, the main downtown artery, The Fix on Sixth attracted a healthy mix of tourists and locals. The bar had existed in one form or another for decades, becoming a local staple, albeit one that had been falling deeper and deeper into disrepair until Tyree had bought the place six years ago and started it on much-needed life support.

"You've never been here before?" Reece asked as he paused in front of the oak and glass doors etched with the bar's familiar logo.

"I only moved downtown last month. I was in Los Angeles before."

The words hit Reece with unexpected force. Jenna had been in LA, and a wave of both longing and regret crashed over him. He should have gone with Brent. What the hell kind of friend was he, punishing Jenna because he couldn't control his own damn libido?

With effort, he forced the thoughts back. He'd already beaten that horse to death.

"Come on," he said, sliding one arm around her shoulder and pulling open the door with his other. "You're going to love it."

He led her inside, breathing in the familiar mix of alcohol, southern cooking, and something indiscernible he liked to think of as the scent of a damn good time. As he expected, the place was mostly empty. There was no live music on Sunday nights, and at less than an hour to closing, there were only three customers in the front room.

"Megan, meet Cameron," Reece said, pulling out a stool for her as he nodded to the bartender in introduction. Down the bar, he saw Griffin Draper, a regular, lift his head, his face obscured by his hoodie, but his attention on Megan as she chatted with Cam about the house wines.

Reece nodded hello, but Griffin turned back to his notebook so smoothly and nonchalantly that Reece wondered if maybe he'd just been staring into space, thinking, and hadn't seen Reece or Megan at all. That was probably the case, actually. Griff wrote a popular podcast that had been turned into an even more popular web series, and when he wasn't recording the dialogue, he was usually writing a script.

"So where's Mike? With Tyree?"

Cameron made a face, looking younger than his twenty-four years. "Tyree's gone."

"You're kidding. Did something happen with Mike?" His cousin was a responsible kid. Surely he hadn't somehow screwed up his first day on the job.

"No, Mike's great." Cam slid a Scotch in front of Reece. "Sharp, quick, hard worker. He went off the clock about an hour ago, though. So you just missed him."

"Tyree shortened his shift?"

Cam shrugged. "Guess so. Was he supposed to be on until closing?"

"Yeah." Reece frowned. "He was. Tyree say why he cut him loose?"

"No, but don't sweat it. Your cousin's fitting right in. Probably just because it's Sunday and slow. " He made a face. "And since Tyree followed him out, guess who's closing for the first time alone."

"So you're in the hot seat, huh? " Reece tried to sound casual. He was standing behind Megan's stool, but now he moved to lean against the bar, hoping his casual posture suggested that he wasn't worried at all. He was, but he didn't want Cam to realize it. Tyree didn't leave employees to close on their own. Not until he'd spent weeks training them.

"I told him I want the weekend assistant manager position. I'm guessing this is his way of seeing how I work under pressure."

"Probably," Reece agreed half-heartedly. "What did he say?"

"Honestly, not much. He took a call in the office, told Mike he could head home, then about fifteen minutes later said he needed to take off, too, and that I was the man for the night."

"Trouble?" Megan asked.

"No. Just chatting up my boy," Reece said, surprised at how casual his voice sounded. Because the scenario had trouble printed all over it. He just wasn't sure what kind of trouble.

He focused again on Cam. "What about the waitstaff?" Normally, Tiffany would be in the main bar taking care of the customers who sat at tables. "He didn't send them home, too, did he?"

"Oh, no," Cam said. "Tiffany and Aly are scheduled to be on until closing, and they're in the back with—"

But his last words were drowned out by a high-pitched squeal of "*You're here!*" and Reece looked up to find Jenna Montgomery—the woman he craved—barreling across the room and flinging herself into his arms.

Meet Damien Stark

Only his passion could set her free…

Release Me
Claim Me
Complete Me
Anchor Me
Lost With Me

Meet Damien Stark in Release Me, *book 1 of the wildly sensual series that's left millions of readers breathless …*

Chapter One

A cool ocean breeze caresses my bare shoulders, and I shiver, wishing I'd taken my roommate's advice and brought a shawl with me tonight. I arrived in Los Angeles only four days ago, and I haven't yet adjusted to the concept of summer temperatures changing with the setting of the sun. In Dallas, June is hot, July is hotter, and August is hell.

Not so in California, at least not by the beach. LA Lesson Number One: Always carry a sweater if you'll be out after dark.

Of course, I could leave the balcony and go back inside to the party. Mingle with the millionaires. Chat up the celebrities. Gaze dutifully at the paintings. It is a gala art opening, after all, and my boss brought me here to meet and greet and charm and chat. Not to lust over the panorama that is coming alive in front of me. Bloodred clouds bursting against the pale orange sky. Blue-gray waves shimmering with dappled gold.

I press my hands against the balcony rail and lean forward, drawn to the intense, unreachable beauty of the setting sun. I regret that I didn't bring the battered Nikon I've had since high school. Not that it would have fit in my itty-bitty beaded purse. And a bulky camera bag paired with a little black dress is a big, fat fashion no-no.

But this is my very first Pacific Ocean sunset, and I'm determined to document the moment. I pull out my iPhone and snap a picture.

"Almost makes the paintings inside seem redundant, doesn't it?" I recognize the throaty, feminine voice and turn to face Evelyn Dodge, retired actress turned agent turned patron of the arts—and my hostess for the evening.

"I'm so sorry. I know I must look like a giddy tourist, but we don't have sunsets like this in Dallas."

"Don't apologize," she says. "I pay for that view every month when I write the mortgage check. It damn well better be spectacular."

I laugh, immediately more at ease.

"Hiding out?"

"Excuse me?"

"You're Carl's new assistant, right?" she asks, referring to my boss of three days.

"Nikki Fairchild."

"I remember now. Nikki from Texas." She looks me up and down, and I wonder if she's disappointed that I don't have big hair and cowboy boots. "So who does he want you to charm?"

"Charm?" I repeat, as if I don't know exactly what she means.

She cocks a single brow. "Honey, the man would rather walk on burning coals than come to an art show. He's fishing for investors and you're the bait." She makes a rough noise in the back of her throat. "Don't worry. I won't press you to tell me who. And I don't blame you for hiding out. Carl's brilliant, but he's a bit of a prick."

"It's the brilliant part I signed on for," I say, and she barks out a laugh.

The truth is that she's right about me being the bait. "Wear a cocktail dress," Carl had said. "Something flirty."

Seriously? I mean, *Seriously?*

I should have told him to wear his own damn cocktail dress. But I didn't. Because I want this job. I fought to get this job. Carl's company, C-Squared Technologies, successfully launched three web-based products in the last eighteen months. That track record had caught the industry's eye, and Carl had been hailed as a man to watch.

More important from my perspective, that meant he was a man to learn from, and I'd prepared for the job interview with an intensity bordering on obsession. Landing the position had been a huge coup for me. So what if he wanted me to wear something flirty? It was a small price to pay.

Shit.

"I need to get back to being the bait," I say.

"Oh, hell. Now I've gone and made you feel either guilty or self-conscious. Don't be. Let them get liquored up in there first. You catch more flies with alcohol anyway. Trust me. I know."

She's holding a pack of cigarettes, and now she taps one out, then extends the pack to me. I shake my head. I love the smell of tobacco—it reminds me of my grandfather—but actually inhaling the smoke does nothing for me.

"I'm too old and set in my ways to quit," she says. "But God forbid I smoke in my own damn house. I swear, the mob would burn me in effigy. You're not going to start lecturing me on the dangers of secondhand smoke, are you?"

"No," I promise.

"Then how about a light?"

I hold up the itty-bitty purse. "One lipstick, a credit card, my driver's license, and my phone."

"No condom?"

"I didn't think it was that kind of party," I say dryly.

"I knew I liked you." She glances around the balcony. "What the hell kind of party am I throwing if I don't even have one goddamn candle on one goddamn table? Well, fuck it." She puts the unlit cigarette to her mouth and inhales, her eyes closed and her expression rapturous. I can't help but like her. She wears hardly any makeup, in stark contrast to all the other women here tonight, myself included, and her dress is more of a caftan, the batik pattern as interesting as the woman herself.

She's what my mother would call a brassy broad—loud, large, opinionated, and self-confident. My mother would hate her. I think she's awesome.

She drops the unlit cigarette onto the tile and grinds it

with the toe of her shoe. Then she signals to one of the catering staff, a girl dressed all in black and carrying a tray of champagne glasses.

The girl fumbles for a minute with the sliding door that opens onto the balcony, and I imagine those flutes tumbling off, breaking against the hard tile, the scattered shards glittering like a wash of diamonds.

I picture myself bending to snatch up a broken stem. I see the raw edge cutting into the soft flesh at the base of my thumb as I squeeze. I watch myself clutching it tighter, drawing strength from the pain, the way some people might try to extract luck from a rabbit's foot.

The fantasy blurs with memory, jarring me with its potency. It's fast and powerful, and a little disturbing because I haven't needed the pain in a long time, and I don't understand why I'm thinking about it now, when I feel steady and in control.

I am fine, I think. *I am fine, I am fine, I am fine.*

"Take one, honey," Evelyn says easily, holding a flute out to me.

I hesitate, searching her face for signs that my mask has slipped and she's caught a glimpse of my rawness. But her face is clear and genial.

"No, don't you argue," she adds, misinterpreting my hesitation. "I bought a dozen cases and I hate to see good alcohol go to waste. Hell no," she adds when the girl tries to hand her a flute. "I hate the stuff. Get me a vodka. Straight up. Chilled. Four olives. Hurry up, now. Do you want me to dry up like a leaf and float away?"

The girl shakes her head, looking a bit like a twitchy, frightened rabbit. Possibly one that had sacrificed his foot for someone else's good luck.

Evelyn's attention returns to me. "So how do you like

LA? What have you seen? Where have you been? Have you bought a map of the stars yet? Dear God, tell me you're not getting sucked into all that tourist bullshit."

"Mostly I've seen miles of freeway and the inside of my apartment."

"Well, that's just sad. Makes me even more glad that Carl dragged your skinny ass all the way out here tonight."

I've put on fifteen welcome pounds since the years when my mother monitored every tiny thing that went in my mouth, and while I'm perfectly happy with my size-eight ass, I wouldn't describe it as skinny. I know Evelyn means it as a compliment, though, and so I smile. "I'm glad he brought me, too. The paintings really are amazing."

"Now don't do that—don't you go sliding into the polite-conversation routine. No, no," she says before I can protest. "I'm sure you mean it. Hell, the paintings are wonderful. But you're getting the flat-eyed look of a girl on her best behavior, and we can't have that. Not when I was getting to know the real you."

"Sorry," I say. "I swear I'm not fading away on you."

Because I genuinely like her, I don't tell her that she's wrong—she hasn't met the real Nikki Fairchild. She's met Social Nikki who, much like Malibu Barbie, comes with a complete set of accessories. In my case, it's not a bikini and a convertible. Instead, I have the *Elizabeth Fairchild Guide for Social Gatherings*.

My mother's big on rules. She claims it's her Southern upbringing. In my weaker moments, I agree. Mostly, I just think she's a controlling bitch. Since the first time she took me for tea at the Mansion at Turtle Creek in Dallas at age three, I have had the rules drilled into my head. How to walk, how to talk, how to dress.

What to eat, how much to drink, what kinds of jokes to tell.

I have it all down, every trick, every nuance, and I wear my practiced pageant smile like armor against the world. The result being that I don't think I could truly be myself at a party even if my life depended on it.

This, however, is not something Evelyn needs to know.

"Where exactly are you living?" she asks.

"Studio City. I'm sharing a condo with my best friend from high school."

"Straight down the 101 for work and then back home again. No wonder you've only seen concrete. Didn't anyone tell you that you should have taken an apartment on the Westside?"

"Too pricey to go it alone," I admit, and I can tell that my admission surprises her. When I make the effort—like when I'm Social Nikki—I can't help but look like I come from money. Probably because I do. Come from it, that is. But that doesn't mean I brought it with me.

"How old are you?"

"Twenty-four."

Evelyn nods sagely, as if my age reveals some secret about me. "You'll be wanting a place of your own soon enough. You call me when you do and we'll find you someplace with a view. Not as good as this one, of course, but we can manage something better than a freeway on-ramp."

"It's not that bad, I promise."

"Of course it's not," she says in a tone that says the exact opposite. "As for views," she continues, gesturing toward the now-dark ocean and the sky that's starting to bloom with stars, "you're welcome to come back anytime and share mine."

"I might take you up on that," I admit. "I'd love to bring a decent camera back here and take a shot or two."

"It's an open invitation. I'll provide the wine and you can provide the entertainment. A young woman loose in the city. Will it be a drama? A rom-com? Not a tragedy, I hope. I love a good cry as much as the next woman, but I like you. You need a happy ending."

I tense, but Evelyn doesn't know she's hit a nerve. That's why I moved to LA, after all. New life. New story. New Nikki.

I ramp up the Social Nikki smile and lift my champagne flute. "To happy endings. And to this amazing party. I think I've kept you from it long enough."

"Bullshit," she says. "I'm the one monopolizing you, and we both know it."

We slip back inside, the buzz of alcohol-fueled conversation replacing the soft calm of the ocean.

"The truth is, I'm a terrible hostess. I do what I want, talk to whoever I want, and if my guests feel slighted they can damn well deal with it."

I gape. I can almost hear my mother's cries of horror all the way from Dallas.

"Besides," she continues, "this party isn't supposed to be about me. I put together this little shindig to introduce Blaine and his art to the community. He's the one who should be doing the mingling, not me. I may be fucking him, but I'm not going to baby him."

Evelyn has completely destroyed my image of how a hostess for the not-to-be-missed social event of the weekend is supposed to behave, and I think I'm a little in love with her for that.

"I haven't met Blaine yet. That's him, right?" I point to a tall reed of a man. He is bald, but sports a red goatee.

I'm pretty sure it's not his natural color. A small crowd hums around him, like bees drawing nectar from a flower. His outfit is certainly as bright as one.

"That's my little center of attention, all right," Evelyn says. "The man of the hour. Talented, isn't he?" Her hand sweeps out to indicate her massive living room. Every wall is covered with paintings. Except for a few benches, whatever furniture was once in the room has been removed and replaced with easels on which more paintings stand.

I suppose technically they are portraits. The models are nudes, but these aren't like anything you would see in a classical art book. There's something edgy about them. Something provocative and raw. I can tell that they are expertly conceived and carried out, and yet they disturb me, as if they reveal more about the person viewing the portrait than about the painter or the model.

As far as I can tell, I'm the only one with that reaction. Certainly the crowd around Blaine is glowing. I can hear the gushing praise from here.

"I picked a winner with that one," Evelyn says. "But let's see. Who do you want to meet? Rip Carrington and Lyle Tarpin? Those two are guaranteed drama, that's for damn sure, and your roommate will be jealous as hell if you chat them up."

"She will?"

Evelyn's brows arch up. "Rip and Lyle? They've been feuding for weeks." She narrows her eyes at me. "The fiasco about the new season of their sitcom? It's all over the Internet? You really don't know them?"

"Sorry," I say, feeling the need to apologize. "My school schedule was pretty intense. And I'm sure you can imagine what working for Carl is like."

Speaking of …

I glance around, but I don't see my boss anywhere.

"That is one serious gap in your education," Evelyn says. "Culture—and yes, pop culture counts—is just as important as—what did you say you studied?"

"I don't think I mentioned it. But I have a double major in electrical engineering and computer science."

"So you've got brains and beauty. See? That's something else we have in common. Gotta say, though, with an education like that, I don't see why you signed up to be Carl's secretary."

I laugh. "I'm not, I swear. Carl was looking for someone with tech experience to work with him on the business side of things, and I was looking for a job where I could learn the business side. Get my feet wet. I think he was a little hesitant to hire me at first—my skills definitely lean toward tech—but I convinced him I'm a fast learner."

She peers at me. "I smell ambition."

I lift a shoulder in a casual shrug. "It's Los Angeles. Isn't that what this town is all about?"

"Ha! Carl's lucky he's got you. It'll be interesting to see how long he keeps you. But let's see … who here would intrigue you …?"

She casts about the room, finally pointing to a fifty-something man holding court in a corner. "That's Charles Maynard," she says. "I've known Charlie for years. Intimidating as hell until you get to know him. But it's worth it. His clients are either celebrities with name recognition or power brokers with more money than God. Either way, he's got all the best stories."

"He's a lawyer?"

"With Bender, Twain & McGuire. Very prestigious firm."

"I know," I say, happy to show that I'm not entirely

ignorant, despite not knowing Rip or Lyle. "One of my closest friends works for the firm. He started here but he's in their New York office now."

"Well, come on, then, Texas. I'll introduce you." We take one step in that direction, but then Evelyn stops me. Maynard has pulled out his phone, and is shouting instructions at someone. I catch a few well-placed curses and eye Evelyn sideways. She looks unconcerned "He's a pussycat at heart. Trust me, I've worked with him before. Back in my agenting days, we put together more celebrity biopic deals for our clients than I can count. And we fought to keep a few tell-alls off the screen, too." She shakes her head, as if reliving those glory days, then pats my arm. "Still, we'll wait 'til he calms down a bit. In the meantime, though …"

She trails off, and the corners of her mouth turn down in a frown as she scans the room again. "I don't think he's here yet, but—oh! Yes! Now *there's* someone you should meet. And if you want to talk views, the house he's building has one that makes my view look like, well, like yours." She points toward the entrance hall, but all I see are bobbing heads and haute couture. "He hardly ever accepts invitations, but we go way back," she says.

I still can't see who she's talking about, but then the crowd parts and I see the man in profile. Goose bumps rise on my arms, but I'm not cold. In fact, I'm suddenly very, very warm.

He's tall and so handsome that the word is almost an insult. But it's more than that. It's not his looks, it's his *presence*. He commands the room simply by being in it, and I realize that Evelyn and I aren't the only ones looking at him. The entire crowd has noticed his arrival. He must feel the weight of all those eyes, and yet the attention doesn't faze him at all. He smiles at the girl with the champagne, takes a glass, and begins to chat casually with a woman who approaches him, a simpering smile stretched across her face.

"Damn that girl," Evelyn says. "She never did bring me my vodka."

But I barely hear her. "Damien Stark," I say. My voice surprises me. It's little more than breath.

Evelyn's brows rise so high I notice the movement in my peripheral vision. "Well, how about that?" she says knowingly. "Looks like I guessed right."

"You did," I admit. "Mr. Stark is just the man I want to see."

I hope you enjoyed the excerpt! Grab your own copy of Release Me … or any of the books in the series now!

The Original Trilogy
Release Me
Claim Me
Complete Me
And Beyond...
Anchor Me
Lost With Me

More Nikki & Damien Stark

Need your Nikki & Damien fix?

Not only is *Please Me*, a 1001 Dark Nights Nikki & Damien Stark novella releasing August 28, 2018, but there's a brand new *full length* Nikki & Damien book coming in 2018, too!

Lost With Me
Stark Saga, Book 5
Coming Fall 2018

Some rave reviews for J. Kenner's sizzling romances...

I just get sucked into these books and can not get enough of this series. They are so well written and as satisfying as each book is they leave you greedy for more. — Goodreads reviewer on *Wicked Torture*

A sizzling, intoxicating, sexy read!!!! J. Kenner had me devouring Wicked Dirty, the second installment of *Stark World Series* in one sitting. I loved everything about this book from the opening pages to the raw and vulnerable characters. With her sophisticated prose, Kenner created a love story that had the perfect blend of lust, passion, sexual tension, raw emotions and love. - Michelle, Four Chicks Flipping Pages

Wicked Dirty CLAIMED and CONSUMED every ounce of me from the very first page. Mind racing. Pulse pounding. Breaths bated. Feels flowing. Eyes wide in anticipation. Heart beating out of my chest. I felt the current of *Wicked Dirty* flow through me. I was DRUNK on this book that was my fine whiskey, so smooth and spectacular, and could not get enough of this *Wicked Dirty* drink. - Karen Bookalicious Babes Blog

"Sinfully sexy and full of heart. Kenner shines in this second chance, slow burn of a romance. Wicked Grind is the perfect book to kick off your summer."- *K. Bromberg, New York Times bestselling author (on Wicked Grind)*

"J. Kenner never disappoints~her books just get better and better." - *Mom's Guilty Pleasure (on Wicked Grind)*

"I don't think J. Kenner could write a bad story if she tried. … Wicked Grind is a great beginning to what I'm positive will be a very successful series. … The line forms here." *iScream Books (On Wicked Grind)*

"Scorching, sweet, and soul-searing, *Anchor Me* is the ultimate love story that stands the test of time and tribulation. THE TRUEST LOVE!" *Bookalicious Babes Blog (on Anchor Me)*

"J. Kenner has brought this couple to life and the character connection that I have to these two holds no bounds and that is testament to J. Kenner's writing ability." *The Romance Cover (on Anchor Me)*

"J. Kenner writes an emotional and personal story line. … The premise will captivate your imagination; the characters will break your heart; the romance continues to push the envelope." *The Reading Café (on Anchor Me)*

"Kenner may very well have cornered the market on sinfully attractive, dominant antiheroes and the women who swoon for them . . ." *Romantic Times*

"*Wanted* is another J. Kenner masterpiece . . . This was an intriguing look at self-discovery and forbidden love all wrapped into a neat little action-suspense package. There was plenty of sexual tension and eventually action. Evan was hot, hot, hot! Together, they were combustible. But can we expect anything less from J. Kenner?" *Reading Haven*

"*Wanted* by J. Kenner is the whole package! A toe-curling smokin' hot read, full of incredible characters and a brilliant storyline that you won't be able to get enough of. I can't wait for the next book in this series . . . I'm hooked!" *Flirty & Dirty Book Blog*

"J. Kenner's evocative writing thrillingly captures the power of physical attraction, the pull of longing, the universe-altering effect one person can have on another. . . . *Claim Me* has the emotional depth to back up the sex . . . Every scene is infused with both erotic tension, and the tension of wondering what lies beneath Damien's veneer – and how and when it will be revealed." *Heroes and Heartbreakers*

"*Claim Me* by J. Kenner is an erotic, sexy and exciting ride. The story between Damien and Nikki is amazing and written beautifully. The intimate and detailed sex scenes will leave you fanning yourself to cool down. With the writing style of Ms. Kenner you almost feel like you are there in the story riding along the emotional rollercoaster with Damien and Nikki." *Fresh Fiction*

"PERFECT for fans of *Fifty Shades of Grey* and *Bared to You. Release Me* is a powerful and erotic romance novel that is sure to make adult romance readers sweat, sigh and swoon." *Reading, Eating & Dreaming Blog*

"I will admit, I am in the 'I loved *Fifty Shades*' camp, but after reading *Release Me*, Mr. Grey only scratches the surface compared to Damien Stark." *Cocktails and Books Blog*

"It is not often when a book is so amazingly well-written that I find it hard to even begin to accurately describe it . . . I recommend this book to everyone who is interested in a passionate love story." *Romancebookworm's Reviews*

"The story is one that will rank up with the *Fifty Shades* and Cross Fire trilogies." *Incubus Publishing Blog*

"The plot is complex, the characters engaging, and J. Kenner's passionate writing brings it all perfectly together." *Harlequin Junkie*

Also by J. Kenner

The Stark Saga Novels:

Only his passion could set her free…

Meet Damien Stark

The Original Trilogy

Release Me

Claim Me

Complete Me

And Beyond…

Anchor Me

Lost With Me

Stark Ever After

(Stark Saga novellas):

Happily ever after is just the beginning.

The passion between Damien & Nikki continues.

Take Me

Have Me

Play My Game

Seduce Me

Unwrap Me

Deepest Kiss

Entice Me

Hold Me

Please Me

The Steele Books/Stark International:

He was the only man who made her feel alive.

Say My Name

On My Knees

Under My Skin

Take My Dare (includes short story Steal My Heart)

Stark International Novellas:

Meet Jamie & Ryan-so hot it sizzles.

Tame Me

Tempt Me

S.I.N. Trilogy:

It was wrong for them to be together…

…but harder to stay apart.

Dirtiest Secret

Hottest Mess

Sweetest Taboo

Stand alone novels:

Most Wanted:

Three powerful, dangerous men.

Three sensual, seductive women.

Wanted

Heated

Ignited

Wicked Nights (Stark World):

Sometimes it feels so damn good to be bad.

Wicked Grind

Wicked Dirty

Wicked Torture

Man of the Month

Who's your man of the month …?

Down On Me

Hold On Tight

Need You Now

Start Me Up

Get It On

In Your Eyes

Turn Me On

Shake It Up

All Night Long

In Too Deep

Light My Fire

Walk The Line

Bar Bites: A Man of the Month Cookbook(by J. Kenner & Suzanne M. Johnson)

Additional Titles

Wild Thing

One Night (A Stark World short story in the Second Chances anthology)

Also by Julie Kenner

The Protector (Superhero) Series:
The Cat's Fancy (prequel)
Aphrodite's Kiss
Aphrodite's Passion
Aphrodite's Secret
Aphrodite's Flame
Aphrodite's Embrace (novella)
Aphrodite's Delight (novella – free download)

Demon Hunting Soccer Mom Series:
Carpe Demon
California Demon
Demons Are Forever
Deja Demon
The Demon You Know (short story)
Demon Ex Machina
Pax Demonica
Day of the Demon

The Dark Pleasures Series:

Also by Julie Kenner

Caress of Darkness
Find Me In Darkness
Find Me In Pleasure
Find Me In Passion
Caress of Pleasure

The Blood Lily Chronicles:
Tainted
Torn
Turned

Rising Storm:
Rising Storm: Tempest Rising
Rising Storm: Quiet Storm

Devil May Care:
Seducing Sin
Tempting Fate

About the Author

J. Kenner (aka Julie Kenner) is the *New York Times*, *USA Today*, *Publishers Weekly*, *Wall Street Journal* and #1 International bestselling author of over eighty novels, novellas and short stories in a variety of genres.

JK has been praised by *Publishers Weekly* as an author with a "flair for dialogue and eccentric characterizations" and by *RT Bookclub* for having "cornered the market on sinfully attractive, dominant antiheroes and the women who swoon for them." A five-time finalist for Romance Writers of America's prestigious RITA award, JK took home the first RITA trophy awarded in the category of erotic romance in 2014 for her novel, *Claim Me* (book 2 of her Stark Trilogy).

In her previous career as an attorney, JK worked as a lawyer in Southern California and Texas. She currently lives in Central Texas, with her husband, two daughters, and two rather spastic cats.

Text JKenner to 21000 to subscribe to JK's text alerts.

Visit www.jkenner.com for more ways to stay in the know!